# Grace

Book 2
The Dreaming Series
by
Jan Reid

ISBN-10: 0994248725
ISBN-13: 978-0-9942487-2-5

## Books by Jan Reid

Deep Water Tears
Book 1 The Dreaming Series

Grace
Book 2 The Dreaming Series

# DEDICATION

This novel is dedicated to the 'lost' ones…

# ACKNOWLEDGEMENT

I must first make mention of the incredibly inspiring NaNoWriMo challenge (National Novel Writing Month) in which participants are given the opportunity and encouraged to write the first draft of a 50,000 word novel between 1st November and 30th November.

Grace: Book 2 The Dreaming Series, is a product of that challenge and whenever I think of 'Grace', I will remember NaNoWriMo (2014) with great affection. Thank you to all concerned.

My gratitude and sincere thanks once again go to Wiradjuri elder Stan Grant (Senr), for authenticating and granting me permission to use the Wiradjuri content (dreamtime stories) in this novel.

My thanks also go to Boyana Petkova, for kindly permitting me to use her exquisite watercolour painting, Tenderness, for the cover.

# AUTHOR'S NOTE

Although this is a work of fiction, I have endeavoured to ensure the authenticity of all Wiradjuri (Indigenous Australian) content through careful research and validation from Wiradjuri elder, Stan Grant (Senr), and in alignment with the book titled, 'A New Wiradjuri Dictionary compiled by Stan Grant (Senr) and Dr John Rudder'.

The names, Binda, Jannali and Darel are the only non-Wiradjuri content. Binda and Jannali are believed to originate from the people of the Ngunnawal (NSW/ACT), and Northern Territory nations, respectively. The language origin of the name, Darel, though aboriginal, is not confirmed at this time of writing. The term 'aborigine' (as opposed to 'aboriginal'), has been used to authentically portray such usage during the era in which the novel is set. No offence is in any way intended by such usage.

In the Epilogue, the (part) account of the history pertaining to Windradyne and the Wiradjuri people was taken from the (full) account at Wikipedia.

*Please Note:* All content (other than mentioned above) is either a product of my imagination or used fictitiously. Any resemblance to actual persons, living or dead, locations or establishments is entirely coincidental, or has been fictionalised.

*'Laugh gaily old man kookaburra - silence the tears of the night.' - JR*

# CHAPTER 1

The next door neighbours are fighting again. Amidst the yelling, Grace stares at the line of shadow slowly creeping up closer to the hook on the wall above the television set. She wonders if she will ever find something to hang on that hook. It's annoyed her for a long time now; a symbol of her uninteresting, barren life, devoid of anything meaningful. It doesn't help that it's positioned so that she looks at it every time she lifts her eyes during the TV ads.

She hears a *thud* on the other side of the dividing wall between her flat and her neighbours, followed by the shattering of crockery and the slamming of a door. She waits. There it is, heavy work boots stomping along the footpath, fuelled by occasional expletives. She grimaces, *broken sleep again tonight.* He'll return from the pub when it finally closes, thumping the same door he slammed when he left before and yelling abuse at his *missus* who has locked him out. She would complain to the police about her neighbours if she knew it would do any good. But, of course, she should never complain.

'You must be grateful Grace. Always be grateful for what you've been given and *show* gratitude,' Susan would say.

It's much quieter now. If she listens intently, she can hear muffled weeping, on the other side of the wall. Sometimes she is not sure which is worse; the fighting or the weeping. Yet, she still prefers it to her life as it was, with Susan and Dennis.

She looks away from the wall and down at the envelope in her hand, resting on her lap. It arrived two days ago. She was surprised when she found it in her mailbox, instead of the usual electricity bill, or junk mail. She had looked at the inscription on the front of the envelope, addressed with her name, *Grace Taylor*, inscribed in neat but disjointed writing. When she had turned the letter over, she had stared at the name of the sender, unable to decide whether to feel elated of fearful. Would the words contained in the letter in her hand cause her happiness or despair? How would she know how she should feel anyway? They had all been the cause of her unhappiness. Were any of them less to blame than the other?

She looks back up to the hook on the wall. The shadow has passed it now. The room is becoming gloomier, like her mood; the remaining sunlight clutching at her shoulders from the window behind her, until it too, vanishes, like a fleeting thought.

She hadn't always disliked Susan and Dennis. And she hadn't always called her adoptive parents Susan and Dennis either. That was only for her private thoughts; something she had started to do since she had moved into her own flat four years ago.

She had found her adoptive sister, Rebecca, sweet and fascinating at first, eagerly spending as much time with her as she could. She still wonders; if she hadn't asked that question that night and remained ignorant of the truth, would things have turned out differently? Would her life have been *normal*? Would she feel she belonged, even if she wasn't as loved as Rebecca undoubtedly was? At least those earlier years had been better times; especially that first month after Rebecca was born. But things were never the same after Grace's tenth birthday. Her last memory of real happiness, ten straight white candles sitting proudly atop her pink frosted coated birthday cake. She closes her eyes and remembers the night when everything changed...

***

She is walking along the hallway to her bedroom when she overhears Susan and Dennis talking softly in Rebecca's room. She stops by the doorway and looks in. They are admiring Rebecca as she sleeps in her bassinet.

"She has *my* lips, don't you think?" Susan whispers as she looks at Dennis with a smile.

"Yes, she does. But she has *my* ears," he replies proudly, as he taps his right ear-lobe with his fingertip.

"What about me? What do I have of Rebecca's, Mum and Dad?" she asks excitedly from the doorway.

They don't reply. Instead, they just look at each other and shuffle her off to bed. She hears them arguing soon after; their muffled raised voices echoing down the hallway from the kitchen. It must be something she has done, but - what? She hasn't done anything except enjoy her birthday, and everyone was happy until she had walked in to Rebecca's room.

She can't sleep. Her head hurts. Surely she has a right to know what she has done wrong. She was ten now, after all; a *big* girl. There is only one way she is going to find out. She creeps out of bed, along the hall and as close to the kitchen as she can get without being seen, so she can hear what they are saying.

"We need to tell her Dennis."

"I dunno, do we really? She hears concern in her father's voice.

"Well, you heard what she asked. What are we supposed to do - *lie?*"

"No, no, we mustn't do that," he responds quickly.

There is silence for a few moments, and then chairs scrape across the kitchen floor. She almost runs back to her bedroom, fearing she will be discovered. But then they talk quieter. She decides they must both be sitting at the kitchen table.

"If we hadn't been blessed with Rebecca, this would never have become a problem," Dennis continues.

"But we have Rebecca now, thanks be to God. And now we must tell Grace the *truth?*" she hears Susan say with conviction.

"What, that she's adopted, or that her *real* mother was half aborigine," Dennis asks curtly.

She doesn't hear any more of their conversation because all of a sudden she doesn't feel safe. She sneaks back to bed as fast as she can and curls up with her teddy bear, while she thinks about what she has just heard. She doesn't understand what they were talking about. What does *adopted* mean? What did her father mean by her *real* mother? And what was an *ab.or.ig.i.ne* anyway? She comes to the conclusion that there must be something wrong with her. And, if Susan isn't her mother, who is?

She isn't left wondering for long. The next day Susan walks briskly into her bedroom while she is lying on her bed, reading. Without hesitation she sits beside her, takes the book from her hands and lays it on the bed.

Susan tells her that in answer to her question the previous night, she doesn't resemble Rebecca in any way because they had adopted her when she was a baby. She then tries to explain what adoption is and tells Grace they adopted her from the Church, because God wanted them to. Grace asks her if Rebecca is also adopted. Susan just shakes her head from side-to-side. Grace is never able to forget what she says next.

"God has blessed us with her Grace, just like he has blessed you by giving you a good Christian home." And of course, predicably, "You must be grateful Grace, and *show* gratitude for what you have been given."

Grace doesn't really understand what Susan means by being adopted, although she tries to look like she does. She tries really hard not to ask any questions too, something Susan has reinforced, many times.

"You should just accept things Grace. Asking too many questions doesn't show gratitude."

But it all seems so confusing to her, not really knowing how babies are born to start with, although she has seen their cat have kittens, so she imagines it must somehow happen like that to grown-ups.

Susan then stands up and is about to leave when Grace asks her, "Mum, what does *ab.or.ig.i.ne* mean?

Grace has never seen Susan hold her breath for as long as she does after she asks her that question. And she seems to go rigid, like stone.

"Where did you hear that word Grace," she asks sternly after she finally expels her breath.

Grace knows instantly that she is in trouble. But she has to answer. She also has to tell the truth, because Susan and Dennis have taught her to always tell the truth.

"I heard you and Dad talking last night," she whimpers.

Susan takes another intake of breath and this time she goes red in the face. Then she gives it to her...

"You are very, very, naughty, Grace. You know it's not good manners to listen to other peoples conversations. And don't go telling me you couldn't help it. I know you aren't able to hear your father and I talking in the kitchen from your bedroom."

Grace is hoping that might be all the reprimanding she is going to get this time, but it seems she has caused a floodgate to open by her question.

"An aborigine is someone with dark coloured skin Grace. We don't associate with them. Your real mother was half aborigine and that's why you were given up for adoption."

"But, my skin is white Mum, like yours. How can someone with dark skin be my mother?" she asks with trembling lips.

Somehow Susan notices how confused and upset Grace is. She attempts to pacify her by sitting back down on the bed again and gently pulling her close. She places her hand softly on top of her head.

"Grace, God has given you to us. You don't need to go worrying about things like that. Just be grateful to God for what he has given you. You know, he even blessed you with your name. The Church named you before they gave you to us. They said it was a suitable name because they knew it would only be by the Grace of God that you would be adopted into a good Christian family. And you were! So, what does that mean Grace?"

"I should be grateful," she sobs.

***

Grace opens her eyes and looks back at the envelope in her hands. It is starting to become rounded at the corners because she has handled it so much during the last few days. There's no point prolonging it any longer…

With a deep sigh, she picks up the letter opener on the side-table beside her and uses it to carefully open the envelope. She pulls out the pages of writing paper and sets the letter opener back onto the table, along with the envelope. She unfolds the paper and reads...

*Dear Grace,*

*Thank you for your letter. I tell you straight off that when I read it the first time, I as happy as the kookaburras laughing in the big tree out back. But I read it many times and I know you been real sad, so I cry for you too. I cry lots of tears for you my daughter, ever since the day you was born, even though I don't know where you was. Every single day I think of you with tears in my heart.*

*Yes, I your mother. You found me! I didn't need you to send that paper that say you was born at Barons Reach. You say you been told that Mary Gilmour work at Jannali a long time ago. You say you writing to find out if we know where she went if she no longer with us. She here! It me! I was Mary Gilmour before I married Don Rutherford. It a long story and I want to tell you and explain things to you properly.*

*Was it old Mrs Bartlett that tell you where she sent me? Don rang her a long time ago for me. He try to find out what happen to you. Old Mrs Bartlett a mean boss. She took you from me all those years ago. I know she wouldn't tell me where you went, even now. But she told Don she didn't know what he was talking about. Maybe you find out from the Church? They wouldn't tell Don anything either. They say they have no records. I so proud of you for looking for me. You make me so happy, but I know I be the happiest person in the world when I see you.*

*I don't write so good so please don't be ashamed of your mother for that. I was taught to read and write at the Home in Cootamundra, but I think I need to tell you all about that when we meet up.*

*I hope more than anything you want to meet me. My heart is aching to hold you, least once. I never got to hold you after you was born. I will write my phone number at the end of this letter if you want to talk to me. If you ring me we can work out where to meet, if you want to. I will be waiting to hear from you, even if you just want to talk.*

*I hope this letter has made you happy my daughter.*

*Your mother,*
*Mary Rutherford.*

# CHAPTER 2

Grace drops the letter on the table beside her, jumps up and rushes to her bedroom. She rummages through her handbag on her bed for some loose change. "Yes!" she announces triumphantly, as she quickly pockets a handful of coins.

She goes back into the lounge room, snatches up the letter, grabs her keys from the key holder in the hallway, and speeds out the front door.

She sprints across the road and turns the corner to the public telephone booth. It's empty. She enters, closes the door behind her, takes a huge intake of breath and expels it. Though her hands are shaking, she punches in the numbers she reads from the bottom of the letter. She can feel her heart thumping in her chest as she listens to the phone ringing down the line. But, with each ring, her resolution starts to wane. Should she have thought more about what she would say before ringing? What if she says something wrong, like she always seems to with Susan? Would it then cause her mother to not want to see her? She looks quickly at the letter that she brought with her and is reassured; her mother wants to see her. She changes gears, dares to believe the phone call will go well; prepares for the best. But no amount of preparation could have ever prepared her for the sheer joy of hearing her mother answer the telephone; "Hello, this be my daughter calling?"

Don, Mary's husband and Grace's step-father, later told Grace that from the moment the letter had been posted, Mary had refused to leave the homestead. She said she had been waiting nearly twenty-three years to hear her daughter's voice, so now Grace had her phone number, nothing was going to stop her from being close enough to answer when she called. And then she had answered the phone in exactly the same way for every call, as she had when Grace had called. Needless to say, until Grace's call came, Mary promptly ensured no-one spoke for very long. "I better hang up. I expectin' a important phone call," she would say down the line.

On their first phone call, after initial sobs of joy at hearing each other's voice, Mary and Grace organised to meet the next weekend for a picnic at the Biddybungie Reserve overlooking the Macquarie River in Dubbo. That had been Mary's idea. It was late on a Sunday when Grace called and although Mary would have jumped in her car and driven to Bathurst to see her straight away, she thought it better to wait until Grace's next day off work. She said she could hold out to the following weekend, if Grace could.

When she later told Don about their plans, she explained that she didn't want to overwhelm Grace with too many new faces to start with. Don had thought that was good thinking, although he was also looking forward to meeting his daughter. From the beginning, he never called Grace his step-daughter. As far as he was concerned, Grace was his daughter. And when he finally met her on the second visit, he felt like he had known her all his life; she was almost a replica of her mother at the same age.

Grace had barely slept that week before their first meeting, and it became quite apparent to her co-workers at the hospital. At first they asked if she were unwell, but once she assured them that wasn't the case, they suggested she must therefore be burning the candle at both ends. They had never seen her looking so tired, yet with a smile on her face and a distinct spring in her step. They also pointed out, her lapses in concentration. After much deliberation on the subject, her co-workers all agreed that given the combination of those things, there must be a new man in her life.

She had just smiled, letting them think they were right. She had no intention of sharing her secret, no matter how hard her co-workers tried to find out. It was something she was going to hold on to; protect from all scrutiny. In any case, at least until she actually met her mother.

Knowing she would soon meet her had not only consumed her mind, but had left her unable to keep her emotions under control also. One minute she found herself smiling from ear-to-ear, and the next, tears were running unchecked down her face. The latter had mostly occurred as she lay in bed trying to sleep each night. Yet, despite, or more likely, *because* of the myriad of emotions she was experiencing, for the first time ever, she had never felt so - alive!

Let everyone think what they like, she had decided. She had enough trouble trying to understand what was going on in both her mind and heart to try to explain it to someone else anyway.

However, although she had hardly slept in the lead-up to meeting her mother for the first time, when the day arrived, she raced out the door of her flat with renewed energy, almost forgetting to close the front door in her excitement. She had then jumped into her dark blue Corolla and zipped through the streets of Bathurst and out onto the open highway to Dubbo, like a racing-car driver.

During the drive, her mind sped along almost in sync with the car motor, churning the information she had so far gathered from Mary, around and around, along with questions that had haunted her for most of her life. Mary had said in her letter that she had tried to find her, but why was she taken from her in the first place? And who was her father, and why did they *let* old Mrs Bartlett take her, anyway?

By the time she pulled up at the Reserve she felt sick in her stomach. She remembered she hadn't been able to eat breakfast before she had left Bathurst. She would have liked to have imagined that was the reason there now seemed to be butterflies fluttering around in the pit of her stomach. But, she knew otherwise. She was nervous; nervous about so many things and mostly about the answers to her questions. Would they be what she needed to hear, could readily accept? Or would they immediately plunge her back into the abyss of rejection and despair she knew so well? How could she have allowed herself to become so vulnerable; permitted herself to hope that meeting her mother would put an end to her torment?

When she stepped out of her car she looked over towards the river and saw a figure moving briskly towards her. She felt unable to move, or even think, and even though the figure was striding purposefully towards her, everything seemed to be happening in slow motion, like in a dream. Then suddenly, her mother was standing in front of her. And it was there at Biddybungie Reserve, she saw her own soft hazel eyes surrounded by long, thick lashes, smiling tenderly back at her. And the butterflies in her stomach immediately disappeared.

No-one could have doubted they were mother and daughter. Their physical resemblance to each other was astounding. They both shared the same height of five foot, nine inches, give-or-take a fraction or two, and a slim, athletic looking build, although Mary possessed a little extra padding around her hips and arms. Those wonderful warm arms that encased her in the most loving embrace she had ever experienced.

Their hair was also the same dark-brown colour, although Mary's was speckled grey in places, and while Grace's long hair fell like ripples of water down her back, Mary's was shorter and more wispy. Though any woman would be jealous of their matching high cheekbones and almost flawless skin, the centre of their beauty lay in their eyes. Anyone who was lucky enough to have their attention would even in some small way feel mesmerized.

Grace had not expected her mother to be as attractive as she was, and especially at her age. Grace would be turning twenty-three in a few weeks. From her birth certificate, she knew Mary had been twenty years old when she had been born. That would mean she was now around forty-three. She could easily pass for someone still in her thirties, especially from a distance, she thought. But noticing the similarities between them, for the first time in her life, she realises why she had never lacked attention from men. It was one thing to stand in front of a mirror and imagine flaws you think others must see, but quite another when you see yourself mirrored in someone standing in front of you. In that instance, because she saw both the similarity between herself and her mother, *and* her mother's beauty, she felt truly beautiful for the first time in her life.

From the time her adoptive parents had told her that her mother was half aborigine she had started to study her body in the bathroom mirror, and half expected to see her skin start turning brown overnight. She also started to look more closely at anyone she noticed with dark coloured skin. After about a year she decided that as she hadn't seen anyone with a mixture of brown and white limbs, that wasn't going to happen to her. And finally, she had reconciled with herself, she couldn't be the *only* one who had a half aborigine mother. Surely there had to be someone she knew from school or church who shared the same secret, and she hadn't noticed anyone else's skin changing colour. Therefore, she needn't worry that it would happen to her. So, she eventually concluded that being *half* aborigine must mean being born with lighter coloured skin.

Sometimes she even imagined that one of the aborigine women she saw around Bathurst was her mother, and somehow suddenly recognised her and took her away. Therefore, by the time she had become a young woman, she was fully prepared for Mary to look like any of the lighter skinned aboriginal woman she had seen around Bathurst. But she would never have imagined that her mother could so easily pass for a white person; the only trace of aboriginality being evident in her honey-coloured skin.

She had wondered at first, if it would have mattered to her if her mother had looked more like a typical aborigine, with darker coloured skin, thick black curly hair and a broad nose. And the very fact that she had felt apprehensive about her mother's appearance, made her feel ashamed. She knew she couldn't change the fact that she had aboriginal blood, but if her mother had looked like a typical aborigine, she wondered if it would have caused her to feel differently towards her. However, although she will never have the opportunity to find out, now that any concerns about it were completely laid to rest, she can't imagine it would have mattered in the slightest, anyway.

Mary had known instinctively, what to do or say, and even what not to do or say. After an initial hug, she motioned for Grace to follow her as she led the way to a picnic spot she had set up for them on the river bank. As they both took a seat at the picnic table looking out at the river, Mary asked her how her trip had been from Bathurst, and if she'd noticed if the orchards were still producing apples as she had passed through Orange. She had planned the small talk, even though instigating it had called for every ounce of self-restraint. She ached to question Grace about her life; find out everything about her. Even the tiniest details would assuage a need she had felt for so many years. But, she knew Grace would have questions she would need to answer before she could ask her own. She was also giving her daughter an opportunity to settle her emotions. Judging by the look on her face, it seemed to Mary that she was having one hell of an internal battle with that. If only she could wrap her arms around her and tell her that everything was now going to be alright. That no matter what had happened in her past, she could look to the future with a promise of better things, because her real mother was going to make sure of that. If only she would start by opening up to her. Speak the truth of her heart.

As if reading Mary's mind, Grace suddenly blurts out, "Why did they take me from you, and why did you let them?"

Mary looks directly into her daughter's eyes. "I tell you daughter, don't worry, but first I need to tell you about things before that. So you understand better, ok?"

Grace nods, showing acceptance.

Mary turns her head, faces the river and watches the water moving slowly downstream. Grace waits patiently while Mary seems to be gathering her thoughts. She turns back to Grace, and looks into her eyes.

"I lost my mother too, when I was 'bout ten. We live in the bush. My mother, she a Wiradjuri woman from around here; The Wiradjuri, our people." Grace nods, pretending to understand. She imagines The Wir-ad-jur-i would probably be a number of aborigines who live in the same area, like a state or country, but she doesn't want to interrupt her mother to ask. "My father, he white, that's all I know 'bout him. I only see him now and then. I think he work at one of the properties 'round here. Anyway, one day the police come an' took me because the government told them to take any half-white children from their aborigine mothers. That's what they did back then. They might still do it…I dunno. They say it to give us half-castes a better life. Hmpf! It all lies; real sorry-business," She pauses, and looks back to the river, deep in thought. She returns her gaze to Grace. "They take me to Cootamundra Home where there's a whole heap of others like me. That place run by the Nuns from the Church. They teach me some white man's education, but it hard to learn. There was no talking our own language. We got belted and locked up if we did. Mostly, they train us for work. They train me to be a Domestic. That what I doing when you was born, daughter. I was working as a Domestic at Barons Reach, in Bathurst."

Mary now scrutinizes Grace's face, considering her next words. She decides to go ahead and ask. "You said you talked to old Mrs Bartlett?"

"Yeah, I didn't have my birth certificate when I moved out of the family home. Susan, that's my adoptive mother, didn't want me to have it, so I didn't have anything to go on at first, to find you. But, I got a job in the office at the hospital and I was able to look through all the records. I had remembered Susan putting my sister's hospital wrist band in a box in a cupboard when she came home from the hospital. Later, after they told me I was adopted, I sneaked a look and found there were two hospital wrist bands. I couldn't read all that well then, but I was able to make out that they both had our names and Bathurst District Hospital written on them. So, by the time I started work at the hospital, I figured there should probably be some sort of record there. That was the main reason I applied for that job in the first place," she says with a wry grin. "That's when I found out that I was born at Barons Reach and that my mother's name was Mary Gilmour."

"You a clever girl, proves you my daughter, hey," Mary adds to try to lighter the mood a little.

Grace giggles at her mother's humour but returns sombrely to her story. "I found out where Barons Reach was and drove out there. I told the house-maid who opened the door after I knocked that I was there to speak to the owner. I didn't know who it would be. The house-maid invited me into the front foyer and asked me to wait while she spoke to the Mistress. I was real nervous Mum, but I knew I had to be brave if I was going to find out anything."

Mary smiles at the way Grace has used 'Mum' for the first-time, and etches it in her memory. "I know you was Grace. That old biddy a mean old thing. She make anyone nervous just hearin' her name."

Grace continues, "Yep, that's for sure. When I was called in to see her I could hardly walk because my legs were shaking that much, even though I hadn't even met her at that stage. She was standing by the fireplace with a walking stick in one hand. I introduced myself and I told her I was trying to find my mother. When I mentioned your name, it seemed to jolt her at first, like I had said something that sort of frightened her. Anyway, she soon got over that because she told me she didn't know anyone by that name and couldn't help me. She then waved her walking stick at the door and said goodbye, dismissing me. Well, I figured I had nothing to lose. I refused to budge even though I wasn't sure what I was going to say next. I was desperately trying to think of something to keep me there longer, to try to find out more. It was then that I noticed she was caressing a gold cross that hung around her neck. I took a stab in the dark that she was a good Christian, a regular church-goer like my…Susan and Dennis. So, I looked her straight in the eye and said: 'I'll leave, but I'll tell you this first. I won't stop looking for my mother, ever! It won't make any difference whether you tell me or not, but if you don't, I'll stand at the door of every church in the Bathurst area and ask if anyone knows what happened to the baby born to Mary Gilmour at Barons Reach. You'd better be prepared for the news to reach you, from well-meaning friends.' And then I turned to leave."

Mary gasps, reaches over and gently squeezes Grace's hand. "Oh Grace, you so bold." Grace smiles softly, appreciating her mother's praise, and touch. "What she say then?" Mary asks eagerly.

"Well, just as I reached the door, she said, 'Wait, don't go!' She then told me that you had left shortly after I had been born, to work for the Rutherfords at Jannali, in Dubbo. That's how I found you. I looked in the telephone directory and found the names, Mr and Mrs Rutherford, Jannali, Dubbo, listed. I wasn't to know of course that *you* were Mrs Rutherford, until I read your letter." Grace sighs. "But, who is my father, and how come you weren't able to keep me?"

Mary had talked at length to Don about what she would tell Grace about her birth, right up until the night before their meeting. However, it wasn't until the early hours of that morning, while she was lying in bed next to Don sleeping soundly and listening to the kookaburras greeting the morning sun, that she had finally made up her mind. She had to protect Grace, at all costs. She already knew her daughter must have had sadness in her life, being without her real mother. In one respect they had both been through similar experiences, although Grace had never known her mother, even if Mary had lost hers also.

Grace did not need to know about her father though. She did not need to know that her father was John Bartlett Jnr, the son of old Mrs Bartlett and her deceased husband, John Bartlett Snr. She didn't need to know that she was conceived through rape, and that John Bartlett Jnr continued to take advantage of her mother, even after her belly had started to swell and she had told old Mrs Bartlett the truth. She hadn't achieved anything by telling the truth. She had been belted for lying and locked in her room every night after she had finished her work. It hadn't made any difference though, because Grace's father had known where the key was hidden, and he had continued to take her as he pleased, right up until her waters broke.

What good could possibly come of telling her daughter about old Mrs Bartlett's only son? Hadn't Grace suffered enough by losing her mother? Wouldn't it be far better for her to never know who her father was, than to know and thereafter feel ashamed of him? She was more than prepared to let Grace think she had been a little wayward, then to know the truth about her father. It was a lie she was willing to take to her grave.

She blinks away tears threatening to escape as she begins to tell Grace about her father. She starts with the truth, but ends with the omissions and untruths which she had rehearsed in her mind earlier, hoping her words sound convincing.

"There lots of white men who work at Barons Reach. Some stay for a long time, but some only for a bit. All the workers made to work hard there, but we all find something we like to do, to keep from giving up. Well, it make me happy to look at the stars. I 'member stories my mother teach me; some, about the stars. It always make me feel peace-like when I look at them. But there no way I can see the stars from my bedroom at Barons Reach. So, one night after I finish my work, instead of going straight to bed, I slip outside with no-one watching. Anyway, I was dreaming-like, looking at the stars this night, when a man came up to me. I nearly panic, straight away thinking I get into trouble. But, he just stand there with me, looking up at the stars. We start to talk about all sorts of things. He seem real nice." She clears her throat. "Well, after a while I decide I better go back inside, but he tell me I beautiful and kiss me. I guess it was 'cause I was lonely, or maybe it was 'cause we both lonely. Anyway, we end up making you under the stars that night. I never saw him again. You were born nine months later."

Mary looks across at Grace. She is looking down at her hands. She leans across and places a finger under her chin, gently encouraging her to lift her head. Grace complies and she looks into her sad, moist eyes. "I so sorry I can't tell you more about him Grace," she says softly, and it takes all her effort to hold back her own tears from flowing.

"So, it was because he left Barons Reach before I was born then…" Grace begins tentatively, "…you couldn't look after me on your own?"

Mary shakes her head. "Back then, if you had a baby 'fore you was married, you 'shamed. But it not the reason for me; it no matter to me, daughter," she says with conviction. "I want so much to keep you; you my baby. But you born white, and my skin still not all white, so old Mrs Bartlett did what those white people always did back then; they took you from me. She was friends with the police and the Church. She knew who to give you to when you was born. I didn't know what happened to you. They wouldn't tell me. I was put on the train to Dubbo two days later. That mean old lady planned it all, a long time 'fore you was born." Mary looks back over to the river, tears now streaming down her face at the memory. "I don't know if you can ever forgive me daughter, for not leaving that place 'fore you was born. If I been able go anywhere else, I would. And I would have hid you from them." She then bows her head and weeps.

Grace moves along the picnic table seat so she is sitting right beside her and reaches over to hold her hand. "Mum, even though there is nothing to forgive, if it makes you feel any better…" she waits for Mary to lift her head and look into her own tear-filled eyes,…"I forgive you."

# CHAPTER 3

Darel wraps his arms firmly around Rachel from behind and nuzzles her neck. She gasps momentarily, but smiles and giggles with delight, grasping the arms encircling her.

"Where did you come from?" she jokingly scolds him.

"I haven't lost my touch then," he smirks.

Grace smiles at them both, watching their familiar banter, and looks away towards the club house. "Is Johno here yet? she asks.

When she receives no reply she looks back at Darel and Rachel. They are now facing each other, kissing.

"Oh, get a room you two." She rolls her eyes, smiling at them.

They disengage, but Darel grins at his sister, and his light blue eyes sparkle. "There's one waiting for us back at the flat Gracie." He looks back into Rachel's emerald green eyes, 'Remember, we're engaged now." Rachel blushes.

Grace knows Darel's not expecting a reply from her, and she couldn't be happier for her brother and future sister-in-law, even if she tried.

She looks away from them, and sits on the wooden bench

beside her. She watches the tennis players milling around the club house, keeping an eye out for Johno, her partner for the spring, night-tennis tournament.

It had been the opposite last year. She had partnered Darel, and Rachel had partnered Johno. But that was before Rachel and Darel had sorted things out. Poor Rachel, she hadn't known then that I was Darel's sister, that he even *had* a sister. She had been so confused.

Grace knows full well what it's like to be confused, like Rachel had been. She also knows what it's like to feel powerless about your life. Yet, they had both succeeded in finding the truth they each sought. And finding the truth had changed both their lives in incredible ways. It had also made them the closest of friends.

Grace's first meeting with her mother had proved without doubt to be the most life-altering for her, and one of the most important moments of her life. She shakes her head as she thinks about it. Sometimes she feels she almost needs to pinch herself to believe it wasn't all a dream.

So much had happened since she had moved to Dubbo. Well, when she had first moved to Jannali, really; a four thousand acre, wheat and sheep property in the Central West Slopes and Plains of New South Wales, just over an hours travel by car, north of Dubbo.

***

After the first meeting with her mother, she returned to her flat in

Bathurst with her mind at peace. Most of her questions had been answered. She couldn't blame her mother for not knowing any more about her father. That was something she would just have to accept; that she would never have the opportunity to meet him, or even know any more about him. At least she now knew who her *mother* was, and she couldn't be happier about that.

Despite her mind being at peace though, she had been physically and emotionally exhausted. Her sleep-deprived body, by then also emotionally drained, finally succumbed. She slept the remainder of Saturday and most of Sunday.

She called her mother again on Sunday night, feeling much more refreshed. She said she just wanted to hear her voice again. At their first meeting Grace had told Mary she would call again soon, but Mary hadn't expected it the next day. She was thrilled. She could tell that Grace was much more relaxed, so she didn't think it would be too soon to ask her if she would like to come back the following weekend, to meet her brother and Don. A second meeting was arranged; this time, at Jannali. It was there she first met Darel and Don.

Darel and Don were both around six feet tall, and it was clear to see that working the land from sunrise to sunset kept them both fit and strong. Don had passed down his curly hair to Darel, although while Don's salt-and-pepper coloured curls were kept under control with major clipping, Darel's were the dark brown of his mother's, and left free to settle wherever they wished. Grace was yet again surprised, this time to find that Darel was just as white as his father, and nearly the image of him.

Don had leaned forward and kissed her on the cheek when she had alighted from her car, and then shook his head from side-to-side.

"What?" said Mary out loud, watching him.

"She's the spittin' image of you Mary," he said with a look of amazement on his face, as he grinned from ear-to-ear. "When she was your age of course though Grace, Mary's got a bit more contentment on her now," he added quickly with a wink.

Mary had pretended to pout and thumped him affectionately on the arm. Grace had warmed to Don straight away.

Darel had welcomed her with a wide grin and said, "Hello Gracie."

She had never liked hearing her name altered that way before, but somehow, it had sounded different, nicer, coming from her brother. So she hadn't said anything. Instead, she had given him a smile in return. Then they had all made their way into the homestead.

When she had first pulled up at the old house, she had not known what to think. It looked like something from a history book. But, although she had been closer to the truth than she realised, she had still been in for a surprise.

Grace was to learn that Jannali homestead was the oldest surviving slab hut house in the district, and possibly even in Australia. Don explained that it was made from timber, bark, clay and all sorts of natural materials. He told Grace that his great grandfather arrived in the area before any other white people, back in 1840. He became friends with the aborigines who lived in the area, and he learned a great deal from them, including from which natural materials to build the homestead. He said he was thinking about asking someone about having it Heritage Listed.

She found the interior of the homestead enchanting. Although it had been updated to accommodate more modern conveniences, it still retained a semblance of old-fashioned charm with an imposing sitting room, tent-shaped plaster ceiling and 1950's patterned wallpaper. Don proudly showed her every room of the house. There were some original furnishings, including an iron bed and campaign chest in the master bedroom. There were also some intriguing colourful paintings on the walls. Don saw her looking at one closely as they passed by it on his tour of the house.

"Your mother painted all the paintings in the house," he told her proudly.

Grace raised her eye-brows, impressed. "The colours are so vibrant."

"Yep, she even made the paint too, from all sorts of things around the property. She's a clever one, your mother," he replied.

The paintings that were hanging around the house reminded her of some others she had seen in the Museum in Bathurst, in a small section specifically for Indigenous art and other items. She had been studying one of the paintings one day, when two white men joined her. One of the men made a comment about the painting they were all inspecting. He said that apparently it was supposed to tell a story, like all aborigine art, although he couldn't make sense of it. So, she knew Mary's paintings were aboriginal art, and that there was a story to each one. They were intriguing as well as beautiful, but she can't imagine she would ever be able to understand the story behind each one, either.

After some morning tea of scones, jam and cream, which Grace ate with gusto, and a good strong cup of Bushels tea, Darel took her on a tour of the other buildings on the property.

The first stop was the sandstone stables complex, which they all just called, 'the shed'. It originally consisted of a blacksmith's forge, coach room, sunken cool room, store room and stable, although Don's father had altered it slightly to include a more modern shearing shed.

Grace listened intently to Darel's explanation of what each area was originally used for. She thought it was all very interesting. "There's so much history here at Jannali, Darel. It's really amazing. To think that our mother is part of it all."

"Oh, Mum is part of a great deal more history than Jannali, Gracie. My great-great grandfather may have been the first white man to settle in these parts, but the Wiradjuri people, who we also belong to through Mum, have been here for thousands of years. It's impossible to know how long really, but Rachel told me she read about it at the Warrumbungle National Park information centre, when she went there on a school camping trip. I think she said the information centre said that the aborigines have been here for more than forty thousand years. She also read about the Rutherford history there too."

"Wow," Grace responded. "That really is something, hey." She thinks back trying to remember if she had been told about this person called Rachel before, but gives up. She wants to know everything she can about her new family. "Who is Rachel, Darel?"

Darel looks slightly embarrassed. "Oh, sorry," he says, smiling softly, and his eyes seem to mist over. "Rachel used to live at Binda, the property next door. We sort of grew up together." His smile now wanes. "She doesn't live there anymore." And then he changed the subject.

She has a strong feeling that Rachel means more to Darel than only as a former neighbour.

She stayed for the night at Jannali, and woke to the sound of kookaburras laughing. Hearing their laughter made her smile. She set off in search of them. She followed the noise to the back door, and walked out to see Mary sitting on a decoratively crafted, wooden two-seater, beneath a huge gum tree, just beyond the verandah. Mary met her eyes and patted the seat beside her. Grace walked barefoot through the glistening grass, bathed in morning dew, to sit beside her.

"Good morning daughter," she said with joy in her eyes.

"Good morning Mum," she replied and leaned across to peck her on the cheek. Just then one of the kookaburras let out a loud rendition of its morning call and Grace and Mary laughed too.

Mary then commenced to tell Grace a story which she called, the kookaburra dreaming story:

*Long time ago, the land very dark, and the emu and the bush-turkey were being mean to each other all the time, throwing the other's eggs high into the sky. The moon and the stars were the campfires of all the sky people. One day, the bush-turkey throw the emu's egg so high, it hit some wood of one of the campfires of the sky people and the spark make fire. The fire grow to light the whole earth, making it warm and colourful. They call it - the sun. After that, the sky people agree to make the sun every day, but they want to be reminded. So, they ask the kookaburra to laugh every morning to tell them. When the kookaburra agree, it then called - brother, and from then on the kookaburra always protected. It important to the people.'*

Just as Mary had finished the story, the kookaburras started laughing again, and Mary and Grace once again joined them.

Later that morning as Grace was packing her overnight bag and preparing to leave to go back to Bathurst, Mary comes into the guest room. "Grace, Don and me want you to know that this is your home now. We your family and always be here for you."

Grace walks over and wraps her arms around her in a hug. "Thank you Mum. That means more to me than you can imagine."

"No daughter, I got good imagination. I know." She pauses, considering whether to voice her thoughts, and decides to go ahead. "Now, I got a thought. But, you don't have to do it if you don't want to."

"Okay. So, what is it Mum?"

"Well, I know you not been too happy in Bathurst. I just wonderin' if you might consider movin' to Dubbo; with Don, me and Darel, here at Jannali. I know you got a job in Bathurst and Jannali might be too far to travel into Dubbo and back every day for work, but Don and me would look after you for a while. You wouldn't need to work while you livin' with us."

"Oh, I couldn't do that to you and Don, Mum. I'd feel like a freeloader."

"Don't you go talkin' like that Grace! You our daughter, you hear?

Grace smiles and nods.

"Anyway, you think about it, ok?"

"Thanks Mum, I will."

Grace did think about it, and three weeks later she arrived at Jannali with her suitcases.

She had returned to Bathurst and looked around her cold, lonely flat, and the hook on the wall, with distaste; concluded her job had served its purpose in helping her to find her mother, and that other than a few acquaintances, she had no real friends who would miss her anyway. She would simply ring and tell Susan and Dennis she had found her *real* mother and she was moving to the Dubbo area to be closer to her. She couldn't imagine there would be much of a response from them about it. They seemed to forget that she existed any more anyway, other than to expect her to attend annual birthday celebrations and Christmas.

She had last seen Rebecca, a few weeks prior, when she had presented her with a birthday present for her thirteenth birthday. Relieved that Rebecca's birthday had fallen on a school day this year, she had decided she didn't need to go to her old home, to be scrutinized by Susan and made to feel inadequate, as usual. She had worked through her lunch-hour at work that day so she could spend that time to see Rebecca instead.

So, she met Rebecca as she was coming out of the school gates, and they walked away from the throng of children converging towards the buses, which waited expectantly for them. There was still a good ten to fifteen minutes before the buses would leave, so she knew she had time.

She pecked Rebecca on the cheek and wished her a happy birthday, presenting her with a gift wrapped in pink and white floral paper and tied with a purple bow on top. Rebecca took the gift and looked tentatively over her shoulder at a group of girls milling near a tree a little further up. She thanked her for the gift, but instead of opening it as Grace had hoped, she quickly crammed it into the backpack she was holding, zipped it tight and said she had to go. Grace watched her turn and race up to the group of girls she had been looking at. They then all walked off a little further up, without a backward glance. Grace hoped Rebecca liked the floral make-up bag inside, filled with an assortment of eye-shadows and lip gloss. But, she would never know. It was clear she wasn't needed in Rebecca's life any more either.

Mary was over the moon when she arrived at Jannali, and Don was not only happy to have Grace with them, but couldn't stop smiling because of how happy Mary was. Darel had given her a big hug and said, "I'm real glad you've come Gracie." She knew she had made the right decision.

Mary said that Grace had timed it perfectly, because she would be able to celebrate her daughter's twenty-third birthday the following week, on February 11th. Grace had been a little surprised when Mary had said that, and Mary had noticed the look on Grace's face.

"Do you think I forget my own daughter's birthday?" she had said seriously to Grace. "Every year on February 11<sup>th</sup>, I wish for you to have a happy birthday daughter. But now my other wish, to be with you on that day, come true. How good is that?" she had exclaimed.

Mary was so excited when Grace's birthday arrived. She presented her with a camera and a photo album, as a birthday gift from them all.

"You got to fill that album with happy memories daughter," she had said with glistening eyes.

After tea that night, she had then proudly brought a birthday cake to the table. While she lit the candles in front of her daughter, Grace had looked at the beautiful flower decorations surrounding the words, 'Happy Birthday Grace', inscribed with pink icing. She had looked up at Mary with tears in her eyes.

"Thank you Mum, this is the best birthday I have ever had."

Following her birthday, Grace's days were filled with helping Mary with the house-work and the gardening; something that brought mother and daughter closer together as the weeks progressed.

At night, Don and Darel often watched television or read, but sometimes Darel joined Mary and Grace as they sat out back under the big gum tree, looking up at the stars. Although Mary had fabricated much of what she had told Grace about the night she had been conceived, she had told the truth about her love of looking at the night sky.

"The stars show us many things Grace," she said on the first night they were star-gazing together. "But, one thing I learn a long time ago. Sometimes people lookin' at the exact same thing, but they argue they different. The stars a good example."

Grace was quickly learning her mother's mannerisms and habits. One she was very aware of was the way she seemed to get a far-away look in her eyes, just before she was about to tell her something pertaining to the Wiradjuri culture. She notices that look on Mary's face now and settles back comfortably in the seat beside her to listen.

Mary points to a section of the sky and Grace follows her gaze. "Can you see them stars there, what people call, the Southern Cross?" she asks.

"Yes, it's that group of stars that look like the shape of a cross, if you join them," Grace replies, as she draws an imaginary line connecting several stars.

"Yep. Now, there are two stars that look like they're pointing to the Southern Cross. Do you see them, there and there?" Mary points to two brighter stars below the Southern Cross constellation.

"Umm, yep, I can see them."

"They's called the Pointers. Don tell me that. He say they point the way to the Southern Cross."

"Oh yeah, I remember being told that now," Grace says, nodding.

"That good you know daughter. Now, them same stars, you know as the Southern Cross, my mother's people call, Mirrabooka." She watches Grace take it in. "And, them stars you know as the Pointers, my mother's people say they are Mirrabooka's eyes, watching over the Earth."

"So, who is, I mean, who *was*, Mirrabooka," Grace asks.

"Ha, you a good girl Grace. You don't know it, but you say the right thing."

Grace frowns, confused.

Mary pats Grace's hand, resting on her lap. "It ok daughter. I tell you and I 'splain in a minute. First though, my mother say, *'A long time ago, there was Mirrabooka. He a kind and wise man, and he look after his people real good. The Creator Spirit, called Biyaami, decide to reward him. He give him eternal life when he die on Earth. When that day come, Biyammi put him in the sky and stretch him along it.'* So, that what some call the Southern Cross, others call Mirrabooka. But they same. See?" she asks.

"Ok, I understand. But, what did you mean when you said I said the right thing before?"

"Stay with me a bit, I get to it, ok? You see daughter, in my mother's culture, everything goes back to the Dreaming. It the time when everything made, but still – is! Many ancestor spirits come to Earth at first. They change into human bodies and move through the land. They make all the different types of land; the mountains and hills, the valleys and rivers, even the rocks and water holes. They make all the animals too. One most important thing they make though was the laws about how everyone should look after each other, and everything they make. And when the ancestor spirits finish, they change into everything they make, except some, like Mirrabooka, who go to the sky. But, they all still alive! That's why I say, good girl - you got it right; you ask who Mirrabooka *is*, first, instead of askin' who Mirrabooka, *was*." She pats her hand again with a big smile. "You see daughter, even though I live with Don and they say we own Jannali and Binda, we don't, not really. But, don't you go tellin' Don I said that," she warns Grace. "Darel knows what I mean. We the caretakers of this land and everyone else who live on land everywhere. We all a part of it. It ok Don look after it too, cause he a good man and he teach Darel to look after it properly." She looks up again at the stars and sighs. "It good I now home, where I started, and where my ancestors live."

Grace leans towards Mary, touching her, shoulder to shoulder. "I'm so glad you were able to come back to your home Mum. Thank you for telling me about Mirabooka."

Mary returns her gaze to Grace. "Good. That a start. Darel and me can both teach you more, cause he learned real good." Mary looks at Grace thoughtfully. "You know, some white people around respect our ways too. That a good thing."

"Hmm, like Don of course," Grace answers.

"Yeah, but also that Bill Winton that used to live at Binda, and his daughter, Rachel." She smiles to herself. "Rachel know our way just like Darel. He teach her too."

"Darel's mentioned her name. I'd like to meet her one day."

"You will, you will," Mary says smiling at her and patting her hand again affectionately.

Over the following months, Mary taught her many things about the Wiradjuri culture, including all the dreaming stories and words she had remembered from her childhood.

Sometimes they went for walks, and Mary explained how various trees, saplings and wild plants were not only once used for food, but for many other purposes too.

The long leaves of rushes and lilies were used to make baskets and mats, or they were soaked and beaten to free the fibres to make string.

The bark of trees was used to make dishes and shields. As they walked along the river bank, she pointed to the river red gums and told her that they were the best trees for making canoes.

Medicines came from the plants too, such as the native mint bush. She told her how it was used to make remedies for coughs and colds, and the leaves were crushed and placed on the temples to relieve headache. The gum from the gum trees, she said, was rich in tannin, and used for burns.

"You see daughter, long time ago, the land give people everything they need. They was taught, even when theys little, how to manage the rivers and land, so they always have plenty."

It was clear to Grace that Darel shared their mother's respect of the land and the Wiradjuri culture. Occasionally he would join them, and he was just as eager to show her things Mary had also taught him. She found it all very interesting, but she wasn't sure she felt an affinity with it, like they seemed to.

Mary had never liked going into town much for supplies, so she was thrilled when Grace offered to do the shopping for her. That way Grace was able to become a bit more familiar with Dubbo and the surroundings, too. She had told Don and Mary when she arrived that she would be eventually moving into Dubbo when she found work there. But, she wasn't in any great hurry. It felt good to be accepted as part of the family; unconditionally. That was something she had never known before.

A few weeks later, Don, Darel and Grace were all eating breakfast, when Don cleared his throat to make an announcement. Darel and

Grace look up from their plates, and Mary walks over from the kitchen counter where she is making her toast and stands behind Grace's chair.

He looks at Darel. "Son, I was planning on putting this to you when you were a few years older, either when you turned twenty-one, or if you married earlier, but..," he pauses, looking at Grace to let her know she is included in the conversation..." I think now's the right time. What do ya think about managing Binda?"

"You mean takin' care of it on my own?"

"Yeah, but reapin' the rewards too; your own property as such. I'll be here to help if you need it, you know that. You'll only be a stone's throw away."

"So, you're suggestin' I move into the house at Binda too?"

"Yep, and Grace might like to go with you, help you out for a while, you know, with the cookin' and cleanin' and such." He looks at Grace. "That's only if you want to Grace," he reassures her. "We're not tryin' to boot either of you out of the house or anything," he adds looking from his daughter to his son and back. "It's just that it's been my plan all along for you Darel, since we took over Binda from the Wintons, to give it to you as a twenty-first present, or even as a wedding present. Whichever came first."

Darel looks to Grace. "It's your call Darel," she says smiling. "I'm more than happy to help you out."

"But, you still come and see me every day Grace," Mary interjects.

"Of course Mum," she answers with a smile, and pats Mary's hand that is resting on her shoulder.

Don looks directly at Darel. "I know you know what you're doing around the property. You're a good worker son. You deserve this."

"I have the best teacher," Darel says as he gets up from the table and accepts his father's handshake.

"So, when do we move? Grace adds, smiling brightly.

Darel and Grace didn't see the private look shared briefly between Don and Mary after that. Don had told the truth when he had said that he had planned to give Binda to Darel, once he turned twenty-one or married, but what he hadn't told them was that he had decided to offer it to him earlier, because of Grace. Darel had only just celebrated his eighteenth birthday a few months prior, but Grace's arrival had caused him to think long and hard about things.

Darel was certainly capable of looking after the property next door. He had been working with him full-time since he brought home his School Certificate at the end of Fourth Form, leaving high school to work with his father on the land, like many other sons of farmers in the district. But, now Mary had found her daughter, he had to think about her too. He knew that although Grace was still getting to know her mother again, she would probably end up getting itchy feet like most young women living on the land. She was also five years older than Darel, and at an age when she would normally be looking for a husband. She reminded him of Mary in so many ways, and he remembers that Mary had been around the same age when he had proposed to her. In Mary's case, worried that she might take off looking for a husband, had prompted him to let her know his true feelings. He had counted his blessings a hundred times over since he had proposed that day, even though Mary later told him that she would have remained his housekeeper to the end.

Grace would end up moving into town, he was sure of it. She had even told them that was her intention. But, he wanted to ensure she knew with certainty that she had roots at Jannali and Binda first. They had all made it known to her that she was wanted, but by offering her the opportunity to help out Darel, it also showed her she was *needed*. It would provide her with a purpose to stay for as long as she wanted.

As for Darel, well, he had a pretty good idea that he would have a bride to bring back to Binda in the near future, if he were given a fair go. He had made sure Darel knew Rachel was still in Dubbo; that she had ended up working in the office at her parents farm supply business, Wallace & Co, part-time between her TAFE classes. If it weren't for Rachel's mother still trying to prevent them from seeing each other, they would be a lot further along in their relationship by now. It was bound to happen though, no doubt there; he had seen it when they were still only tots. He reckoned Darel and Rachel would sort it out sooner or later. In the meantime, managing Binda would keep him busy, and having a sister to introduce to Dubbo would get him into town often enough, where he would have the opportunity to see Rachel.

Yes, he feels he has covered all bases.

On the evening of the day they moved across to Binda, Darel and Grace sat on the back verandah watching the last rays of the sun glistening on the river through the river gums. Grace notices that Darel is deep in thought. She had noticed at times over the last few weeks that he sometimes looked like something was bothering him;

particularly when he came back from a trip to Dubbo. She had grown quite close to her brother in a very short time. She cared about him and she was concerned. She decided she was going to ask him about it, but as if he had read her thoughts, he started talking about it before she could bring it up.

He began by telling her about Binda. He said it was a three thousand acre property, which had once belonged to the Wintons; Rachel's family. He said her parents had sold it to Don when a large tree branch, called a 'widow-maker', had fallen on her father and injured him. He hadn't been able to work the land after that. That's why Rachel had ended up in town. Both Jannali and Binda had belonged to Don and their mother since then, although the Rutherford family had owned both those properties and several others, before Don's grandfather had sold them off over a hundred and fifty years ago.

Darel told Grace that things had been difficult for Rachel. First she had been sent to boarding school in Orange, when she was only eleven, going on twelve. Then her parents had sold Binda and moved into Dubbo a few years later. After she left boarding school she ended up helping her parents in operating a farm supply business. It had been a huge change for her. She had missed Binda desperately all the time she had been at boarding school, and she had said that she only just managed to cope with it because she knew she would be able to return to it one day.

"She didn't like boarding school you see Gracie. She used to tell me all about it during the school holidays. She did make a few friends, one of them called Jess, but for the most part I think she just felt like a duck out of water." He pauses, remembering, smiling... "That was, unless she was on a camping trip, like the one she went on at the Warrumbungle National Park. That was where she read all about Mum and Dad's family history." His smile evaporates as he continues. "Rachel and I grew up here in the bush together; separated only by the dividing fence, over that way." He points to the north. "There's this huge gum at the end of the fence, close to the river bank. That was our meeting place. We would meet near that gum tree every day after primary school and on the weekends when we were little. But, we still met there during Rachel's boarding school holidays too." He smiles again, remembering, "We'd go swimming in the river in the summer, walk through the bush and always find something interesting. I taught Rachel all the Wiradjuri dreaming stories and words I know, and told her about things in the bush. Like Mum and I told you," he added, looking at Grace briefly to acknowledge her, before returning to his memories. "She was always so interested; always wanted to know more. When we were little, I taught her how to walk quietly in the bush and creep up on someone, although she always had a habit of making a big racket when we were playing tag. She nearly trod on a brown snake once; it was so close. When it rained, I'd build a lean-to or we'd climb trees, thinking we'd be able to stay dry. But, we usually ended up pretty wet, so we'd take off down the track to the Jannali shed. Most of the time though, Mum found us, and took us inside the homestead to dry off. Hmm, then she was sent away to boarding school. I always knew when she'd arrived home for holidays though. I could just tell, and I'd be waiting for her at the dividing fence. We did a lot of sittin' and talkin' by the river in those days. Hmm, but then the time came when she went back to boarding school and her parents moved into town…" Grace notices his eyes welling up with tears, although he turns his head to try to hide them. "I miss her," he says, as if talking to himself, gets up and walks inside.

Grace knew she didn't need to reply. He had just needed someone to listen.

***

Still thinking about the last eighteen months, Grace looks towards Darel and Rachel again. Darel is now playing with Rachel's long golden wavy hair. He seems mesmerised by it. She turns and puts her arms around his neck. When she sees them this way, Rachel's deep emerald green eyes gazing into Darel's sky blue eyes, Grace thinks it is one of the loveliest things she has ever seen. She could not in any way be envious of the love Rachel and Darel share. She could only dream that she would be as fortunate one day.

Darel and Rachel join her on the bench. She suddenly notices her right leg is numb from sitting with it tucked underneath herself. She stands and walks back and forth around the bench in an attempt to get rid of the pins and needles she now feels.

"You got ants in your pants, Grace," Johno says, behind her.

She turns to scowl at him playfully, but pauses when she comes face-to-face with a man standing beside him she has never met before.

"Hello, I'm Dan, Dan Matthews," he says, looking deeply into her eyes, and time stands still.

# CHAPTER 4

"His *brother*…but he doesn't look anything like Johno," Grace exclaims as she follows Rachel up the steps to their flat.

Rachel smiles to herself. "Nope!"

"Well, I guess that happens," Grace mutters, following Rachel through the front door.

Rachel turns to look at her, giving her a cheeky grin.

"What!" Grace retorts.

"Nothin'," Rachel answers with a giggle.

Grace continues walking to her bedroom at the far end of the hallway. She leans her tennis racquet against the wall beside the wardrobe and hangs her back pack on the hook behind the door. She walks back out to the lounge room as Darel comes through the front door.

"So, good night, huh?" Darel says, looking at Grace, grinning.

Grace bends over to pick up a cushion from the lounge to throw at him in response to his obvious teasing, but Rachel distracts them both.

"Ok, hot Milo you two? she asks, holding up the can of Milo from the other side of the kitchen counter.

"Yes please," they both say in unison. Rachel turns to the kettle to hide a smirk.

Rachel and Darel chat about the matches they played that night while she makes the hot drinks for them all. Grace appreciates how Rachel has tactfully changed the subject, but she decides she needs to be alone. She picks up her drink from the kitchen counter as Rachel picks up the remaining two mugs and heads to the lounge where Darel is sitting. She casts them both a quick look as she heads out of the room.

"Thanks Rachel, night."

"Night Grace," both Rachel and Darel respond, in unison.

She walks slowly along the hallway to her bedroom, being careful not to spill the warm chocolate drink on the carpet. She puts the mug down on the bedside table, sits on her bed and removes her tennis shoes. She adjusts the pillows against the bedhead, leans back on them, and relaxes.

She knows Darel and Rachel won't mind being left alone. They were most likely already cuddling on the lounge and talking about their wedding before she had even made it to her bedroom. She picks up the mug and swallows a mouthful, savouring the taste of the warm chocolate as it glides down her throat.

They had only just become engaged, announcing it at a family dinner, two weeks ago, at Jannali. Rachel said they had chosen February 14th as their wedding date because it would fall on a Saturday in 1981.

Mary, Don and Grace had all been thrilled with their news, although Don reminded Darel that they could bring the date forward if they wanted to, now that he was living at Binda. Darel had cast a quick look in Rachel's direction, and unspoken words passed between them. Darel had then said that there were several reasons they had chosen that date, and although it would be hard not seeing each other every day, the wait would be worth it. Don had nodded, accepting his son's response without further question. Mary had then announced that they needed to toast the occasion, and went off in search of a bottle of wine and wine glasses. Don had followed, to assist.

It had then suddenly dawned on Grace, one of the reasons for their chosen wedding date.

"Oh, how romantic – Valentine's Day," she had exclaimed, as she raced around the table and gave them each a big hug.

When Mary and Don came back with the wine and wine glasses, Rachel told them all that they wanted to have the wedding ceremony on the grassy spot by the river, at the dividing fence; their favourite place. And they only wanted a small wedding, with family and a few friends. Rachel had looked across the table at Grace, who had returned to her seat by then, and asked, "Grace, would you be my Maid of Honour?"

"Oh Rachel…but, what about Jess? She's been your friend a lot longer than I have."

"You're my good friend too Grace, as well as family, the sister I always wanted. And don't forget, you'll officially be my sister-in-law after the wedding. Besides, I need my Maid of Honour close by to help me plan and choose things, even if it's only going to be a small wedding. Jess will understand, and she'll probably be relieved you're here to help me, because she's always so busy at uni. But, we will need to get her to visit soon now, because I want to ask her in person to be my bridesmaid. I don't want to do it over the phone." She bites her bottom lip, deep in thought and then her face suddenly lights up. "Here's a thought, Darel's entering the Wood-Chopping event at the Show next month. How about I try to get Jess and Martin to visit then, use the Show as an excuse, and then surprise her with the news?"

It had warmed Grace to hear the excitement in Rachel's voice.

"That sounds like a great idea," she had replied.

"So?" Rachel had looked at her with raised eyebrows.

"So, what…oh yes, of course I'll be your Maid of Honour. Thank you for asking me."

Rachel had later told Grace that when she had told her own parents, Betty and Bill Winton, about their engagement, the response had been entirely different. Well, her mother's response at any rate. Although her mother had never been shy in voicing her opinion, Rachel said she hadn't counted on her almost having a seizure because of the news. Her father, on the other hand, had smiled the broadest smile and hugged his daughter with sincere joy and congratulations. However, it had taken almost a full hour for Rachel and Bill to settle her mother down, at least to a more tolerable, tearful and sullen mood.

Grace had asked her why her mother had reacted that way. Rachel had suddenly looked startled, as if remembering something. She had then looked back at her thoughtfully, while she chewed on her bottom lip; a habit Grace had begun to recognise she did when she was unsure about something.

"Well, Mum's always been a bit of a snob," she had finally said with a forced chuckle.

Grace hadn't questioned her any further, because Rachel had then quickly changed the subject; another habit she was becoming familiar with. Rachel had the ability to quickly steer a conversation away from anything which may cause anyone, including herself, any embarrassment or concern.

However, she now wonders why she had reacted that way to her question. They had both openly shared many personal things since they had become friends. But then, neither of them had spoken much about their mothers, or in Grace's case, her adoptive mother. Perhaps Rachel was embarrassed by her mother's behaviour, and just didn't want to dwell on it. She could easily relate to that.

After all, it was obvious to anyone that Darel was a great catch. Grace knew she wasn't being biased because Darel was her half-brother. He came from a well-known, respected family, and was well-liked in the community. He was a hard-worker and stood to inherit a very sizable property. He loved Rachel deeply and would do anything to make her happy. And, to top it off, he had his father's chiselled good looks and wide easy smile. Surely any mother would consider him suitable for her daughter? Especially when it was obvious how much she loved him too.

She takes another mouthful of her warm drink. Jess will be coming for a visit soon. The thought makes her smile. It was always fun when she stayed with them, even if they were just sitting around, talking.

When Jess visited, she stayed with Rachel and Grace at the flat, and slept on the futon that Rachel had bought at a garage sale soon after Grace had moved in to the second bedroom. It served well as a second lounge and as a bed when it was unfolded.

If Jess's boyfriend, Martin, came to visit also, he would stay at Johno's flat, on the other side of town. Martin and Johno had both been friends at boarding school too, at the brother school to where Rachel and Jess had been.

At some point, they would all end up together, at least for a meal at the club. Although Grace was around five years older than Rachel and Jess, and even Darel, Martin and Johno, it didn't make any difference to their friendship. They all got on so well together.

When she first met Jess, she was surprised at how different she was to Rachel. While Rachel was generally quiet by nature and tended to be more a listener than a talker, Jess was the complete opposite. She effortlessly became the life of any gathering and her infectious laugh often had them all in stitches, sometimes for no other reason than she had started to giggle in the first place. Grace found it fascinating that although the two friends were so different in nature and lived hundreds of kilometres apart from each other, they were so close. At first she thought it was because of the years they had spent together at boarding school. But, on a later visit from Jess, when the women had decided to have a girl's night-in, and had drained several bottles of wine, another reason for the closeness of their relationship became apparent.

Grace had only been making conversation at the time; showing an interest in Jess's life. She hadn't meant to pry. But, when she asked her how long she had been with Martin, she would never have imagined she would learn that Martin had originally been Rachel's boyfriend. They had met at one of the inter-school dances, and then remained together in a long distance relationship, right up until Rachel and Darel finally sorted things out.

Grace had been at Binda the day Rachel had come to say a final goodbye to Darel. At that stage, Rachel hadn't known that she was Darel's sister. So, although it had been obvious to her that Rachel and Darel had always loved each other, it came as a surprise to Grace to hear that she had been Martin's girlfriend. She couldn't imagine them being together, at all.

As Jess had spilled the beans, Rachel had teasingly reprimanded her, and told her to set the story straight for Grace. She said she didn't want Grace to think she had been unfaithful to Darel. Jess had laughed at her then, telling her that there was no way she had ever been unfaithful to Darel when she had been with Martin. Rachel had then said that the truth was then, that she had been unfaithful to Martin.

Jess had then leaned over and squeezed Rachel so hard in

a hug that Rachel had cracked up laughing. Through Jess's drunken lips, Grace then deciphered that Jess had pushed Rachel into becoming Martin's girlfriend. It had happened after Rachel had lost touch with Darel, when her parents had moved into town. Jess said that at boarding school, she had always had a *thing* for Martin, but Martin had always had a *thing* for Rachel. So, as it was driving her mad watching her friend self-destruct in mourning over Darel, she gave her a little shove in Martin's direction. If she couldn't have him, then she thought he would be able to at least make Rachel happy. Then it all became quite complicated, with Darel coming back on the scene and Martin discovering at uni that he had far more in common with Jess than Rachel. But, it all turned out exactly as she had hoped in the end, and she couldn't be happier for Rachel, or herself, she had added, as she started on a tirade of hiccups.

Grace decided, that although Rachel and Jess were several years younger than she was, they showed a maturity well beyond their years, and incredible loyalty to each other.

The next time they were all out together, she had looked at the two couples, Rachel and Darel, and Jess and Martin, with far greater understanding of the close bond they all shared.

Johno's involvement with the group had started at boarding school, where he had become friends with Martin, and consequently met Rachel.

When Grace had first met Johno, it was obvious by the attention he gave her, and the way he looked at her, that he had more than friendship on his mind. He was great to be around; always full of fun and making everyone laugh. He did have a more serious side though too, and a casual but effective way of getting you to open up, especially when there was something bothering you. He could be a good listener. But, Grace could never see herself going out with him. She enjoys his company, but only as that of a friend, and she knows Johno now accepts that too.

As grateful as she is for the friendships she had made since moving to the Dubbo area, she wonders if she is destined to be on her own. She hadn't really thought about it that way, until now.

She'd had her share of going out with losers, in Bathurst. For the most part, she'd discovered they had only wanted one thing, and she had quickly walked away. But, it also had had a lot to do with how she had thought about herself too; that she didn't deserve any better. She had been her own worst enemy. She hadn't felt beautiful, even though men had told her repeatedly. She had thought their compliments had only been a tactic they had used to try to win her affection. In fact, she'd felt quite ugly, especially on the inside. She realises now, that Susan and Dennis had contributed to that. But, that was before she met her mother, Don, Darel and Rachel; also, Jess, Martin and Johno. They had all been an integral part of reshaping how she thought about herself. She now felt she belonged, that she mattered, and that had changed her whole outlook on life. She smiles to herself. Even by just announcing their engagement, Darel and Rachel had caused her to now feel that she too was ready to meet someone special. And she thinks about the man she has just met.

As much as she tries not to, she can't get Dan out of her mind. Even after that woman named Jasmine had interrupted their introduction, and made a point of claiming him. He had seemed a bit embarrassed by that she remembers. Perhaps it's just that he doesn't like displays of affection. But then, she had to admit, Jasmine was really over-the-top with her body language, grabbing his arm and brushing up against him while he was talking. Darel and Rachel might canoodle a bit, but there was a difference. Why was it different though? She imagines the two couples side by side. Yes, that's it - it was mutual with Darel and Rachel. Oh, what is she doing? Dan is definitely - hands-off. But, those eyes! How was she ever going to be able to get them out of her mind? She shakes her head. Why did she start thinking about him?

When she had turned around earlier tonight at the tennis club after hearing Johno's voice behind her, she must have looked like an idiot, jumping around trying to get rid of her pins and needles. And she remembers having a pretend scowl on her face. She must have made a terrible first impression. But, so what? She probably won't see much of him anymore, anyway, other than possibly every Wednesday night at the tennis comp for the next few weeks.

Brothers? She was still finding it hard to get her head around it. Could one, or both of them, be adopted? Well, Johno couldn't be; he looked too much like his father. She had spotted his father when she had dropped her car off at Golden West Holden for a service a few months ago. Rachel had recommended the dealership because Johno worked there as a mechanic, and that was where she had her car serviced. She had told Grace that the business belonged to Johno's father, and Grace had recognised Johno's father behind the service desk when she had dropped off her car. There was no mistaking those dimples, along with the same hair and eye colouring. But, she still can't get over how different the brothers are in appearance. Perhaps Dan took after his mother. It wasn't that Johno was bad-looking by any means. Being a little more than average in height, with auburn coloured hair, hazel coloured eyes and a healthy lean physique, Grace imagines he would probably be considered quite good-looking by most women. But when he turned on the charm he took the spotlight; his most attractive feature being his cheeky smile, along with his witty sense of humour. Any girl he managed to catch could never complain about being bored, that was for sure.

Dan, on the other hand, well, he was just your classic, tall, dark and handsome hunk, with muscles that should be outlawed. And those *eyes*. She was amazed she had been able to talk after he introduced himself. His eyes had held her spellbound. Well, that was until Jasmine had come along.

When he had spoken to her, introducing himself, she had frozen. It had taken the voices of Darel and Rachel behind her, saying almost in unison, *Hi Dan*, to bring her back from wherever he had taken her during those few seconds. She had then found her tongue and responded, "Oh, Hi, I'm Grace."

What followed next was a bit of a blur. Once again, just like the day she had first met her mother at Biddybungie Reserve, it had all happened so suddenly, although just prior it had seemed like it were happening in slow motion. Perhaps in Dan's case though, it was because she had been absorbed in his eyes. However, when she thinks more about it, she realises there really isn't anything extraordinary about his eyes. They were attractive, a mixture of light and dark brown, but not all that uncommon. She frowns, contemplating, until the answer appears. Perhaps their most compelling feature didn't really have much to do with his eyes in themselves, but the way he used them.

As soon as they had introduced themselves, Jasmine had appeared. Grace hadn't been left in any doubt that she was Dan's girlfriend. Jasmine had made sure of it. She had seemed to come out of no-where, sidling up to Dan while glancing at Grace condescendingly.

"Oh Dan, so this is where you got to. We're wanted on Court 5. Time to flex those delightful muscles of yours," she had oozed as she had run her hand up and down his arm while pressing her body up closer, and eyeing Grace. "So, who do we have here?" she had asked, with raised eyebrows.

Dan had looked at Jasmine then with a look of annoyance and carefully disengaged himself from her hold. "Grace, this is Jasmine, Jasmine, Grace," he had said, looking strained. She recalls mumbling something about being Darel's sister, not wanting to sound impolite, although she had known Jasmine's question hadn't been uttered with polite intent. Dan had then looked a little defeated, but added, "Well, it was nice to finally meet you Grace," before turning around and striding away with Jasmine half skipping to keep up.

They had all started their first tennis match for the night then. Rachel and Darel had been sent to Court 2, while she and Johno to Court 4. She hadn't played well at all that first match, but she's sure it had nothing to do with Dan and Jasmine playing on the court beside her. She had just needed to warm up and get to know her partner's play better. It had after all been a year since she last played, and last time she had played with Darel. She apologised to Johno several times though when she missed several easy returns. Johno had rolled his eyes at her the first time she had been hit on the shoulder by the ball being returned by their opponent.

"I know, I know. I'll try harder," she had said to him, thinking he had been justified because of her incompetence.

"No Grace, it's fine. It's just that you remind me of Rachel last year, when you were playing with Darel," he had said, chuckling.

It had taken Grace a few minutes to understand what he had been talking about. "He's with Jasmine, Johno. Anyone can see that," she had responded firmly.

"Hmm, yep, it looks that way," he had said, leaving her to refocus on the match they were playing.

She hadn't known then, that Dan was his brother. Why hadn't he told her? For that matter, why hadn't Rachel or Darel told her?

Well, she hadn't really said anything about him, or asked any questions to find out. Johno, Darel and Rachel had all just seemed amused for the remainder of the night every time they interrupted her thoughts. She hadn't given them any indication that she had been interested in Dan, had she? Well, that was until she had asked Rachel about him as they had climbed the steps to their flat. It seemed Darel had noticed things on his own.

Well, it had definitely been an interesting night. But she now makes a promise to herself; she won't let anything distract her next week the way Dan and Jasmine had tonight.

She finishes her drink and decides not to take her mug out to the kitchen. She doesn't want to disturb Rachel and Darel. She likes to give them their space when Darel's at their flat, and she tries not to disturb him while he's sleeping. She knows full well how hard he works; the long hours he puts in. He will be up early, on the road back to Binda long before either she or Rachel wake up in the morning to get ready for work.

She likes her position as a receptionist and administration assistant at the Dubbo Medical Centre. It feels good to know she is helping people, and most of the people she works with are friendly. She gets along well with most of them.

Many of the patients seem to be fond of her too; especially a couple of elderly people who insist on speaking to her when they call to make an appointment. They often say she is the only one who knows which doctor they need to see and the best time for their appointment. In truth, Grace thinks it's probably only because she is a good listener and doesn't rush them off the phone.

She prepares for bed and slides between the sheets, positioning the bedclothes over her arms. She tries to quieten her mind. She reminds herself of how life can change in the blink of an eye. It had happened to her after finding her mother, moving to Jannali, and then Dubbo. So far all these things had occurred, suddenly, without much warning. Would that also be the case when the right man came along? She would be twenty-five next February. Time was passing by more quickly now. She would like to be in a relationship, to feel the way Rachel does. But just when she is about to drift off to sleep…What did Dan mean, it was nice to *finally* meet her!

# CHAPTER 5

The week leading up to the next tennis night dragged for Grace. It hadn't helped that it had been a slower than normal week at work, especially with the quiet weekend in between. Perhaps the warmer weather, heralding the beginning of spring, had obliterated all the winter germs. It wasn't really the case, but she had felt that everything she was doing was a count-down to her next tennis match, and she had wished she had been busier so she could keep her mind from it.

On the weekend, after doing some cleaning and washing with Rachel she had taken off to the library, in search of a novel or two. By then, Rachel had left to drive to Binda for the remainder of the weekend, so she had plenty of quiet time to herself, especially to read. She had deliberately not looked in the romance section at the library. There was no need to remind herself of what she was missing, she had brooded. But, as it turned out, both books she borrowed, 'The Thorn Birds' by Colleen McCullough, and 'Sara Dane' by Catherine Gaskin, contained sad overtones of unrequited love. They were not exactly conducive to the current state of her heart. However, the main characters were both strong women who fought tenaciously for their survival and family, she had consoled herself. Perhaps she had chosen well after all.

She hadn't found out anything more about Dan, after Rachel told her he was Johno's brother. She had been tempted to ask, certain Rachel would know at least something about him. After all, she had known his brother for many years. And besides, in country towns the locals seem to know everyone, or at least, *about* them.

If she had asked Rachel, she would at least have had an insight into the type of person he was. She imagined he would be a nice person; he was Johno's brother. But then, like appearance, it wasn't always the case. Rachel and Darel had seemed pleased to see him though. That was something she knew neither of them would fake. And she trusted their assessment of people.

She hadn't asked Rachel about Jasmine either. She remembered that Rachel and Darel hadn't said anything to her that night, or she to them. In fact, she had been so busy claiming Dan that she had paid little attention to anyone else; except Grace. She had had some experience with that type of reaction though; knew it quite well. There had been occasions in Bathurst where a man had approached her and a jealous girlfriend had been miffed. Though she had often felt complimented by the attention, she had just as often felt sorry for the girlfriend, so she had quickly given the man the brush-off, then watched the jealous girlfriend sigh with relief, or give her man the deserved silent treatment. But, she had felt differently when Jasmine had reacted the way she had. She still can't understand why.

If Jasmine hadn't been in the picture though, she would have pestered Rachel, and even Darel, for information about Dan. They were two people she trusted completely, and she knew they would both keep her confidences. It would have been good to have both a female and male opinion of Dan, even though she would end up forming her own, regardless. But she had no desire to tread on another woman's territory. She was a relative newcomer to Dubbo and the last thing she wanted was for her name to be associated with anything scandalous. She had family now, and she would be devastated if she embarrassed them by becoming the cause of gossip in the community.

She decided then, that she would do her best to keep her interest of Dan to herself. If Dan approached her again she would find out more about him in her own way. She would try to avoid looking into his eyes though, at all costs. Perhaps they may even become friends. That is, if Jasmine would give her a chance. Who knows, Jasmine might even end up being nice once she realised that Grace wasn't trying to lure her man. Somehow she doubts it though…

Wednesday finally came around. It was a beautiful spring night, even warmer than the previous Wednesday. Grace had brought her jacket but doubted she would need it, either on or off the court. They had all turned up at almost the same time. Rachel and Darel had then left to find out which courts they were all playing on. Johno had just sat beside her on the bottom bench of the wooden viewing stand. They both looked towards the town lights beyond the furthest tennis court.

"I reckon we'll smash 'em tonight Grace," he says enthusiastically, glancing at her.

Grace leans back and crosses her arms. "Well, I'll try harder to pick my game up. Hopefully that'll make a difference."

"Aww Grace, you play well. I saw you last year. You just had a few things on your mind last week," he says, turning sideways to look at her again.

There's an awkward silence and Grace sneaks a look at his face. At that moment he smiles gently and turns his face back to the town lights again.

"You know you can ask me anything. Especially about, *anyone*, I know," he says softly.

Grace chides herself for having made her interest in Dan, obvious, even though she had been unaware that she had. But she hasn't *said* anything, and if she finds out all she wants to know, then perhaps she can get Dan out of her mind. She must be careful not to give *too* much away though.

"So, Dan is your brother? Is he the only one, or do you have other brothers or sisters too?"

Johno faces her fully now. "No, just Dan. He's the eldest. He works at the Council; in Building and Development. I think he has a bit to do with Heritage Listing. He's done pretty well for himself. He told Dad he didn't want to work at the dealership, even though that's what Dad expected. He said he had other plans, and next thing you know, he's working at the Council."

"Are you close?" she asks tentatively.

"Pretty much, I guess. We've always got on well even though we don't see all that much of each other. Remember, I was at boarding school for a while? Dan didn't go. And now he lives in the north side of town. Owns his own place; well, started payin' it off anyway. We don't see much of each other because of work I guess – long hours."

From what Johno has said, Grace can see that Dan is the type of man who knows what he wants and works hard for it. However, although Johno has sounded sincere when praising his brother, she's also noticed something she recognises filtering through; a slight envy. That's a little how she had felt with Rebecca, even though she was younger. Perhaps he feels a bit dejected because he's living in the shadow of his brother.

"Hmm, he's done alright for himself by the sounds of it." She cocks her head to the side and smiles at Johno. "But, I think it's nice that you work for your father; you know, keeping it in the family. Who knows, you might end up running the place yourself one day."

Johno gives Grace one of his most charming grins.

Grace considers asking Johno about Jasmine but decides against it. She's found out enough for the time being without looking desperate for it. Besides, Darel and Rachel return and tell them they are needed on Court 6.

Grace is totally stunned a few moments later when they meet their opponents on Court 6; Dan and Jasmine. Well, she decided she wasn't about to let Johno down again, like last Wednesday, no matter what. She would just pretend it were Rachel and Darel on the other side of the net and try to relax. They all walk to the tennis net to toss for first serve.

"So, we meet again," Dan says to Grace, attempting to entrap her with his eyes. Grace remembers her earlier resolution, and only glances fleetingly at his face, with a quick smile. The toss is in their favour, so Johno elects to serve first.

Grace works hard at staying focussed on the game. Johno is able to man the base line, while she intersects the ball in the middle of the court, by either returning strongly to a lob, or strategically dropping the ball just over the net.

She manages to avoid Dan's eyes for most of the match, although she is acutely aware of his presence. She imagines she feels him watching her, especially when she turns her back to bend over and pick up the balls.

She also notices that Dan seems to serve more softly to her as opposed to how Johno does to Jasmine. She imagines Dan is probably just being a gentleman, and serves softer to every female opponent. And although Johno may serve harder to Jasmine, it was nothing compared to when he was serving to his brother. It was definitely, open slater, when Johno and Dan were serving the ball to each other. She was glad she was the female partner of the pair. She probably would have just stood to the side to avoid being hit, and given away the point, if she had had to receive those serves.

She was proud of Johno for holding his own against his brother though, whether it was a quick powerful serve, or a long arduous rally. She imagined they had competed against one another all their lives; sibling rivalry.

They eased into the game, neither pair saying much at all, except for Jasmine egging Dan on when he was rallying with Johno.

"Ohhh, good one Dan. That's the way," she'd say, as she hopped back and forth in the same spot.

It started to get on Grace's nerves, and strangely enough, it looked like Dan felt the same. Grace began to notice that he ignored her, only acknowledging her comments sometimes with a quick word of, *thanks*. She also noticed that he turned away from her with a frown, more often than not, when the play was over.

By the time they were almost half way through the match, they all concurred that the game score was 4-3, in Dan and Jasmine's favour. Then it was Dan's serve. Grace overheard Jasmine saying to him as she handed him the balls, "Ok Dan, enough fooling around. It's time to get serious."

Dan first served to Johno, and aced him. He then looked at Jasmine as if to say - *happy?* Jasmine responded to his look with a smirk on her face.

Next it was Grace's turn. Dan served to her, even softer than he had earlier throughout the match. She returned it well, hitting it back to him in a smooth action. Dan reciprocated. Johno remained at the baseline and Jasmine at the net on the other side. Dan and Grace continued to rally to each other, almost like they were just having a hit of tennis for fun, rather than being in a competition. Jasmine had tried to intersect the rally several times by now, but Grace and Dan had both skilfully kept it just out of her reach. The frustration on her face was becoming quite obvious. Grace momentarily looks at her, and loses her rhythm. Next thing Jasmine intersects her return to Dan, and with all her strength behind her, slams it back at Grace with a grunt.

It happened so fast. Grace hadn't seen it coming. One minute she is starting to really enjoy herself, and the next moment it feels like a rock has hit her in the stomach. She drops her racquet and immediately clutches her stomach as she bends over in pain.

All of a sudden Johno is by her side, asking her if she is alright. She tries to straighten up but finds it too difficult. She looks to the side to see two sets of male legs, which could only belong to Johno and Dan. *How did Dan get here so quickly?* She carefully straightens and looks at the two concerned faces beside her.

"I'm ok," she says, embarrassed. "Just a bit winded," she adds.

"Do you want to stop?" Dan asks.

"No, no. But thanks. Look, I'm ok now," she says as she bends down and picks up her racquet. Her stomach still hurts, but the discomfort is beginning to subside.

"Ok, if you're sure," Dan says, still looking at her, concerned. He then turns his head and glares at Jasmine, who hasn't moved from where she had been when she had sent the torpedo at Grace.

"Sorry Grace," she says, without any tone of sincerity. "But you really should keep your mind on the game," she adds with a smirk.

Dan returns to his side of the net. He resumes his serve, but plays it less vigorously, even when serving to Johno. Jasmine does not look impressed when he loses his serve.

The match then became, dead even, 4-4. It then became obvious that Jasmine was very irritated, and hell-bent on winning. It seemed she had either saved the best till last, or somehow became possessed with inhuman strength and agility. Grace lost her serve, even though Johno had risen to her defence, and attempted to save her from having to run to the ball as much as possible. With a 5-4 lead, Jasmine continued her assault, until finally, the ball landed on the base line just out of reach of

Johno's outstretched arm, and the match ended at 6-4.

"Yes!" Jasmine said loudly, with a smug look on her face.

They all meet at the net then, to shake each other's hands in good sportsmanship. Dan reached for Grace's hand first. She almost jolted when a tingle run up her arm as he clasped her hand in his. It seemed to Grace that if he couldn't get her to look into his eyes, he would make her pay attention to him another way. She didn't want to let go, but Jasmine was sending spears her way, so she had no other alternative. Jasmine then quickly brushed her hand with Grace's. Now Grace knew what people meant when they said it felt like shaking hands with a limp, dead fish. Johno shook her hand firmly, and beamed.

"Good work partner, we nearly got them."

Jasmine and Dan started to walk off the court first, but halfway to the gates he said something to Jasmine and held back, until Johno and Grace caught up to him. Grace noticed Jasmine turn and briefly glare at her then, but she quickly averted her eyes.

"You've got a good partner there Johno," he said, but looked at Grace. She blushed.

"Yep," Johno answered, with a slight grin, although he continued to look ahead.

"Grace, I hear you work at the Medical Centre…."

By the time they made their way to the court gates, Grace and Dan were chatting away amicably. Johno makes his way into the clubhouse, leaving them to continue their conversation alone. They stroll over to the wooden bench and sit side-by-side.

Dan had by now already asked her about her work and if she liked it, and if she played any other sport than tennis. He said Johno had mentioned a few weeks back that he was partnering Darel's sister in the tennis comp. So, that explained why he'd said it had been good to *finally* meet her. She wondered how much Johno had told him though. She wasn't all that keen to divulge too much information about her personal life, especially about being adopted. And, although finding her mother had changed her life dramatically for the better, she was still trying to wrap her head around being part aboriginal. As far as she knew, the only people aware of both these things were her mother, Don, Darel, Rachel and Johno.

Besides, she had a different surname to Darel and her mother, so until it became widely known that she was his sister, and Mary's daughter, no-one would be any the wiser. She reassures herself that she wasn't deliberately trying to withhold that information because she didn't want to be associated with them. She loves them both very much and cannot imagine having a better brother or mother. It's just that she hasn't found it easy to trust people since Susan told her when she was ten that she was adopted. She just feels she needs a bit more time to work things out in her mind before she allows her background to become common knowledge.

Dan said he hadn't seen her around town before last week at tennis, and he wondered where she had been hiding. His question had sounded like he was just being genuinely curious, but she was still a little hesitant. She was also relieved though too, because it looked like Johno hadn't told him much.

She replied, "Well, I was in last year's tennis comp with Darel. Did you play last year? I don't remember seeing you then, either."

"No, I didn't play last year. I had a busy year at work. That would be another reason why I haven't seen you around before, no doubt."

She then felt a little guilty for not fully answering his question. He was being polite and only showing interest. He seemed to become a little downcast when she had avoided disclosing more. It wouldn't hurt to tell him a bit more, she decides.

"I lived in Bathurst for most of my life. I only arrived in the area at the beginning of last year," she said quietly.

He nodded, acknowledging he had heard, but remained silent. He seemed to understand that she didn't want to be asked any further questions.

She then decided it was time to change the subject, anyway. "But what about you, Dan? And Jasmine? How long have you been together?" *Nothing ventured, nothing gained,* she thinks.

Dan clears his throat. "Well, for starters, Jasmine is just a friend. Well, rather, her father is a friend of mine. Her father was my boss when I first started at Council. He's semi-retired now, although still a Councillor. We keep in contact." He laughs. "I think he uses me to keep up-to-date with what's going on. No, not really. In reality, I owe him a lot for helping me to get a start at Council," he concludes.

"So, you became friends with Jasmine through her father," Grace confirms, as she looks squarely into his eyes for the first time since they've sat down.

His eyes pull her into his private space. It is here she sees the truth of his words. "Yes," he says firmly.

Later that night, when she is walking towards her car to leave, Dan approaches her.

"Grace, I was wondering…well, that is, I'm going out to see Don Rutherford on Saturday. It's to do with work; a Heritage Listing for the Jannali homestead. I've already arranged to meet him. I'm wondering if you'd like to come for the drive with me. That is, if you're not busy."

Grace suddenly remembers Don telling her he was thinking about getting the homestead Heritage Listed when she first visited Jannali.

"Hmm, yeah, I guess," she falters not wanting to sound too eager, although she's bursting inside with happiness.

Dan smiles. "Ok then, how about I pick you up at your place. I know where you live. Would around a quarter to nine be ok? I told Don I'd be there at ten."

"Yes, that sounds fine. A quarter to nine on Saturday. See you then," she says smiling as she turns, gets into her car and drives off.

When she pulls up at the flat, she wonders how she made it home at all, because she can't remember concentrating on her driving. In her mind, she had already been with Dan, driving out to Jannali.

# CHAPTER 6

Grace leans back against the brown leather passenger seat of Dan's Jeep Cherokee. He watches her buckle her seat-belt and then starts the engine. He had arrived at exactly a quarter to nine. She had been ready and waiting for about an hour, but she wasn't going to tell him that. She didn't want to seem like a school-girl on a first date, even if she felt like one.

He asked her how her stomach was, and she reassured him that it was fine now. When he had told her last Wednesday night that Jasmine was only a friend, she had felt liberated. She no longer needed to worry that she was treading on another woman's territory. As far as she was concerned, finding that out from Dan had more than paid back for Jasmine's attempt to harm her. There was no proof that Jasmine had deliberately hit the ball into her stomach. To an onlooker it could have easily been an accident. But, it seemed that even Dan hadn't been convinced of that, and she was his partner. It had back-fired on Jasmine though, regardless, and ended up serving no other purpose than to give Grace, Dan's sympathy vote. And then he had invited her to go with him today.

After discussing Wednesday night's tennis, she asked him about his work. Although she had gleaned a little from Johno, she didn't let on that she even knew that much. He seemed pleased she asked, and he obviously enjoyed his work, because they talked about it for almost the entire trip. She didn't mind at all, because it gave her the opportunity to relax, sit back and occasionally look at his profile, or catch a glimpse of his eyes as he sometimes turned to see if she were listening.

He said he was a Planning Duty Officer. His job entailed a number of things, though mainly answering questions regarding: general building enquiries, pre-lodgement advice, preparing certificates, such as a DA - Development Application, a CC - Construction Certificate and Property Certificates, to pre-consultations for Heritage Listings.

He paused to look at her reaction, and because she seemed to be waiting for him to continue, he did. "For most types of development, an application is required to be submitted to Council for approval. Up until recently there was a fair amount of flexibility within the permitted guidelines, but the new Environmental Planning and Assessment Act, just passed, has changed that, and Dubbo Shire Council's new LEP, that's – Local Environmental Plan, now controls more of what you can and cannot do on your land."

Grace interrupts him. "It all sounds so complicated. But it's still interesting," she adds, not wanting to discourage him from the topic.

Reassured he isn't boring her, he continues. "Yeah, it took a while to learn it all that's for sure. I had a good mentor though, which helped a lot."

"From what I've heard Dan, you should give yourself more credit.

Johno told me you work hard, and that's saying something, considering Johno often doesn't leave the workshop until after seven most nights. That's why he's usually running late for tennis. On that note...," she looks at him, waiting for him to look her way.... "do you always work on a Saturday?

"No, not every Saturday. To tell you the truth though Grace, this is definitely more pleasure than work," he says, casting a grin her way. "But, I'm returning Don's enquiry in person." He puts his fingers to his lips. "Shhh, don't tell anyone."

"Hmm, I know it's none of my business, but..."

"Promise me you'll keep it to yourself. Cross your heart?" He watches to make sure she crosses her heart, but she deliberately crosses her fingers to annul the promise, with a cheeky grin, making sure he sees her doing it. He makes a face to look like he is horrified, and she giggles.

"No, I promise, seriously," she says.

"Ok, but I don't need you to promise. You look pretty trustworthy to me," he says, smiling gently. "Darel called in and saw me at Council a few weeks ago. He said Don wanted to know more about Heritage Listing. He said he's been thinking about it for a while; about the Jannali Homestead."

"Yes, he mentioned that to me once too," Grace adds.

"Well, I'm not an assessor, but I can make an appointment for an assessor to come out and see him. From what Darel said to me though, it seems like Don just wants to know more about the process first. I've dealt with a lot of landowners in the community and a lot of the time they prefer to talk about it with someone they know first. They just want to know the facts before they go wasting anyone's time, especially their own. So, I can at least give Don some basic information and let him think about it."

"That's really good of you Dan. I mean you could have just called him, if you didn't want to send out some information in the mail, instead of driving all the way out to Jannali," she said, "...on a Saturday."

"Oh don't worry, that's not the only reason I'm driving out to see Don," he says, with a wide smile. Although he hasn't confirmed it with his words, Grace blushes from Dan's hint that it has something to do with her, and she turns to look out the window at her side.

She gazes at the country side, at the patterned paddocks they pass; the vibrant yellow canola and the green hues of summer wheat, swaying in the breeze. Further away, the hillsides are covered by the rich purple carpet of Pattinson's Curse and bright yellow daisies, dotted with the white specks of lambs frolicking close by their mothers. *Spring is such a beautiful time of year*, she thinks. Her attention is suddenly brought back to the roadside as a flock of Rainbow Lorikeets take to the air, startled from their perches in a gum tree close by.

"They're so colourful, aren't they," Dan says pulling her from her thoughts. He must have been observing her. She looks over at him, and catches his eyes before he turns to look back at the road.

"Yes, my mother has a painting of them at Jannali. She's a wonderful artist," she says proudly.

"So, does it run in the family?" he asks curiously.

"Oh no, Mum's the talented one."

"Hmm, maybe you just haven't discovered your talent yet."

"May-be," she says, but doesn't give it any further thought.

"So tell me, what's this Heritage Listing thing all about?"

"Well, basically, it's a way of protecting a property against losing any of its original structure, especially if, in Don's case, he or someone else plans to further develop. It's also about maintenance, and there is what's called, 'The Local Heritage Assistance Fund' which is offered on an annual basis to provide financial support for owners of Heritage Listed items, to undertake routine maintenance."

"Oh okay…I can understand now why Don is interested. He's so proud of the Jannali Homestead. I know he would absolutely hate it to fall into disrepair. Have you seen it before?"

"No, I haven't. I'm really looking forward to it."

"Yes, well, I have no doubt that an assessor will put it on - 'The List'," she says confidently. "It's very, very old, and I'm looking forward to hearing Don tell you all about it," she says cheekily.

"So, I'm going to get the grand tour, without having to ask?"

"Most definitely," she says grinning.

They see the sign of the village, Barwon, up ahead.

"Well, it looks like we're almost there," he says as he puts his foot on the brake to slow down. "It's been a while since I was last out this way. Where is Wilson's Lane?"

"Just the other side of Barwon. You'll see the turn-off just past the show-ground. So, you invited me so I would make sure you didn't get lost, huh?"

"Oh no, as I said earlier, I have other motives."

"Well, am I going to find out what these 'other motives' are?" she teases.

"Hmm, possibly," he says, casting her a mischievous look.

She is suddenly thankful they've reached the turn-off. She suddenly feels very hot and winds her window down. Despite the warmth of the breeze, she cools instantly.

Dan concentrates on the dirt track they are now on and she decides not to distract him. There are quite a few pot holes on this track that need to be skilfully avoided. She looks ahead and watches for all the familiar sights which indicate they are almost at the Jannali front gates; the old weathered shed on a neighbouring property, the huge boulder underneath the sprawling wild rose bush, and Jannali's white painted barrel mailbox up ahead.

"There it is," she says pointing to the mailbox. He slows and turns into the property, through the welcoming open gates, and follows the track, lined with aged gums and poplars to its end at the Jannali Homestead.

Mary is already out the front waving her hand, even though the dogs would have only just started to bark. Grace giggles and pokes her arm out the window and waves back. Dan stops and they both get out. Grace walks briskly up to her mother and they cuddle each other. And then Mary turns to Dan.

"So, you be Dan?" she asks him with a serious look on her face.

"Yes, Mrs Rutherford."

"No, no. No – 'Mrs' for friends of Grace. My name Mary, ok?"

Dan smiles broadly. "Okay. It's very nice to meet you Mary."

"Alright, now come, come. Don is coming. He must be hold up in the back paddock, but he usually on time for things," Mary explains as she takes off towards the front door of the homestead.

Dan pauses, drawn to look at the outside of the Homestead as Mary leads the way inside. Grace notices the look of fascination on his face.

"See, I told you," she can't help but say. She then walks ahead of him through the front door, breathing a big sigh of relief. She had noticed that Dan had greeted her mother with nothing but complete respect. She frowns slightly, knowing at that moment that she must have been concerned about it, unconsciously.

Don appears, and he and Dan shake hands, amidst his apology for not meeting them when they drove up. He says he lost track of the time. Dan tells him there was no need to apologise as they were probably early. Don walks over to Grace and gives her a big hug.

"Good to see you Grace. Your mother's been complainin' these past couple of weeks that she hasn't seen you for a while."

Grace looks to her mother. "Oh Mum, I told you two days ago when I called that I was coming out today. So, here I am!" She looks at Dan briefly. Earlier in the week, she had planned to drive out and stay for the weekend, but Dan's mid-week invitation had changed that. So, she had called her mother and told her she would be coming to see her, but only for the day.

"Yeah, but it's only for a bit, this time. When you gunna come and stay the weekend again?"

"How about next weekend then?" But then she suddenly remembers…"Oh no, I can't come then. Jess is coming to visit for the Show," she says, feeling a bit guilty. "I'm sorry Mum. How about I come the weekend after that? I'll even come straight after work on Friday and stay until early Monday morning." She pauses, but smiles broadly with a new thought. "Better still, I haven't taken a day off all year. Why don't I take Monday off and stay till early Tuesday morning. That way we can have four nights together?" she finishes excitedly. She's glad she has thought of that because she hasn't seen her mother for a while, and she's missed her.

"That be real good daughter. I knows you been busy, but, yeah, that be real good. You forgiven," she replies, much brighter now and pecks Grace on the cheek as she ushers them all over to the kitchen table to sit down. "Ok, Grace you can help me with the mornin' tea. Grab the cream from the fridge."

She turns to Dan who has just started talking to Don, and interrupts. "Sorry Dan, but just checkin', I hope you like scones, jam and cream?"

"Oh yes, I certainly do Mrs, ahhh – Mary. Thank you."

"Good, good. Let's get this sorted then Grace," she says, and while the men are talking she sidles over to Grace, gives her a big grin and whispers, "He a good fella Grace."

During morning tea, Dan explains all about Heritage Listing to Don. Don listens intently, asks questions that Dan answers clearly without hesitation, and nods when he understands. Mary and Grace half listen to the men's conversation, but generally catch up on what they have been doing since they were last together. Grace also tells Mary how Rachel has invited Jess to visit the next weekend and she is going to surprise her with her engagement news. Mary occasionally glances at Dan, and gradually a frown of confusion forms on her brow. Grace starts to wonder what is bothering her. Just when she decides to find out by using the excuse of asking Mary to show her the new garden she had planted, Mary interrupts the men's conversation.

"Sorry to butt in, but Dan, you work in this Council place most of the time?"

"Yes, I do Mary," he answers.

"Every day?" she continues.

"Ahh, yes. Except most Saturday's and Sunday's," he answers, looking a bit perplexed by Mary's question.

"Hmm, well I just wonderin' how come you got them big muscles when you be sitting down most of the time?"

"*Mum!*" Graces admonishes her, obviously embarrassed.

Don just smiles, but Dan laughs uproariously, unable to contain it. When he finally manages to regain control of himself, he answers.

"Well Mary, I keep fit by lifting weights at the gym in town, the Fitness Centre, and jogging at least three times a week. I play a bit of tennis and cricket too."

"Hmm, Ok, I guess that 'splains it," she says looking less confused but adds, "You know, it seems a bit of a waste, lifting things for no reason. You can come and help Don lift some wheat bags instead, whenever you want - to keep them muscles strong."

Grace hangs her head, determined to avoid Dan's gaze. She's one hundred per cent certain her face is bright red.

Dan chuckles a little, but controls himself this time. "Well, I'll keep that in mind Mary. Thank you for the kind offer."

Don looks fondly at both Mary and Grace, and smiles.

Mary nods, seems satisfied.

Grace stands abruptly. "C'mon Mum, we'll leave them to it. I want to see that new garden you've been talking about."

Grace follows Mary through the back door, and outside to where a new patch of pansies stand erect in all their different patterns and colours.

"Oh, they're so pretty Mum," she exclaims.

"Yep," Mary says proudly. "They sure do make my day sunny when I see them. That remind me, I also plant some sunflower seeds over there," she says, pointing to a patch of cultivated ground near the old gum tree.

"Sunflowers are my favourite flower Mum."

"Well, how 'bout that!" Mary responds, delighted. "That real good then daughter. Soon, when we sit under the tree you will see them. Good, good," she says with a big smile on her face.

At the mention of the tree, they both make their way over to it, and sit beneath its branches.

"You know, this my favourite place at Jannali," she says to Grace. "The kookaburra's favourite place too; they here every morning and every night. You know daughter, the kookaburra our totem," she says nodding her head, looking directly at Grace, ensuring she has taken notice of what she has just said. "They knows it too. That why they be with me in the tree above where I sit."

Grace remembers finding her mother here the morning after she had first stayed overnight, when the kookaburras had been laughing, and all the times they had star-gazed from where they now sat. "I'm not surprised Mum. It's one of my favourite places now too."

What other favourite place you got?"

"Biddybungie Reserve, overlooking the river. 'Cause that's where I first met you," she says without hesitation.

Mary's eyes instantly well up with tears, although she smiles gently and nods her head.

"Yep, that a real good place Grace," she says, remembering their first meeting. "You know, that same river, Macquarie they call it, that the same river that pass through here - it seen a lot of things Grace, that river, a lot of things," she says wistfully as she seems to float away in thought. "It real deep too, 'cause there's been a lot of tears cried in it." Grace remains quiet, allowing Mary to reflect without interruption, but suddenly she returns to the present. "I think we best go see how that man of yours is doing," she says, grinning.

"Mum! He's not 'my man'," she whispers as they stand.

"Hmm, not yet maybe but, you see - you see," she says patting Grace's arm affectionately.

The back door opens, causing the women to look towards it. Don and Dan appear, glance over to them, and stroll towards them.

"Well, I can't see there being any problem Don," Dan says, as they reach Mary and Grace.

Don is nodding, looking relaxed, so Grace decides it must have all gone well.

"I'll be in touch as soon as I make the appointment," he says, holding out his hand to Don.

Don clasps Dan's hand firmly. "Very good, and thank you for coming." He turns to Grace. "Well Grace, I didn't get to see much of you today, but we'll see you in a few weeks."

"Ya goin' so soon Dan?" Mary intercedes.

Don replies, "Now Mary, you'll see Grace soon and I'm sure Dan has things he wants to do for himself now, being a weekend an all."

Mary nods her head dejectedly, but seems to accept it with as much grace as she can.

On the way back to Dubbo, Dan talks about the Jannali Homestead, detailing all the unique historical aspects of it. "It's fascinating," he says, looking deep in thought, obviously remembering the tour Don had given him.

"Yes, it is," she says proudly.

Dan then changes the subject. "Do you have any plans for tonight?"

Grace is momentarily thrown. "Umm, no, nothing concrete, she says," hesitantly. She hadn't even thought past this drive with Dan today. "Why?" she asks.

Dan clears his throat. "Well, I was wondering if you'd like to have dinner with me?"

"Oh, ok. Yes - thank you. That sounds nice."

Dan turns to smile at her briefly. "Is there anywhere you'd like to go in particular?" he asks.

"No, well, I don't really know many places. We, that is, Rachel, Darel, Johno and I, usually just go to the club every so often. It's relaxed, and the food's not bad."

"Hmm, would you like to try somewhere different?

"I don't mind Dan. You choose."

"Ok then, how about the Quality Inn, at the Blue Lagoon motel."

"Ok, sounds good. I'll meet you there.

 "I can pick you up if you like," he says.

Grace decides that even though she's sure she'll enjoy her night out with Dan, she wants to remain independent. Just in case. "Thanks, but I'll meet you there if you don't mind."

He smiles softly. "No problem."

***

Grace's first date with Dan would stay long in her memory for several reasons. Candlelight would now remind her of the way Dan had looked longingly at her through the aura of the flames in their darkened private alcove. Savouring food would now remind her of the way Dan had enticed her to try portions of his meal, bringing his fork to her lips, and watching intently for her reaction to its taste. But, the memory that would outshine all others, would be the way Dan had lifted her hand with gentle reverence to his lips, and kissed her fingertips as he looked tenderly into her soul.

He had claimed her connection then, through his touch and his eyes. She had felt taken to a place she had never been before, a place where nothing else mattered than remaining within that connection.

And at that moment, she knew she would never be the same again.

# CHAPTER 7

The Dubbo Agricultural Show was an annual event looked forward to by the population of the town of Dubbo and the surrounding communities, for many different reasons.

For well over a hundred years, this three day event, showcased agricultural production from the region, promoted businesses to the regional community, and provided competition and entertainment.

There would be thousands of visitors, with various assortments of umbrellas or raincoats, walking through the gates of the town's Showground on Saturday, 6th October 1979; Grace, Dan and their friends among them.

Every year, the preceding days or even weeks would herald brilliant sunny spring weather, but without fail, on the day of the Show the heavens would mysteriously open and bless the event with rain.

Grace had been to the Bathurst Show as a child. Her favourite parts had been Sideshow Alley and the Pavilion. In Sideshow Alley, for the cost of a dollar or two, she was given an opportunity to test her luck and skill by dropping ping pong balls into the mouths of clowns in the hope they would fall into a winning number slot, or try her hardest to knock over canisters with a ball. Though the biggest prize, a huge bear or some other unrecognisable creature, sat teasingly in pride of place at the back of these stalls, a small plastic toy prize was the usual score. However, it was fun and there were always the Dagwood Dogs, Saveloys encased with fried batter, dipped in tomato sauce, and pink Fairy Floss, afterwards. To top it off, if her stomach could take it, she would be taken for a ride in the Ferris Wheel, and at the highest point she would stare in awe at the showground and beyond.

As she grew older, the Ferris Wheel gradually lost its appeal, replaced by more exciting rides such as the Dodgem Cars or the Cha-Cha. But by the time she was old enough to go on them, Rebecca had been born, and her parents were no longer interested in taking her to the Show. However, if she had kept out of trouble during the previous weeks she would sometimes be permitted to tag along with her school friends.

The Pavilion was always the height of activity. At the entrance there would be a stall of Show Bags, and when she was younger and she had been especially good that year, she was permitted to choose one. It had always been a difficult choice. Should she choose the Barbie Show Bag which contained among other items suitable for a young girl, a pair of Barbie glasses, a Barbie colouring book and coloured pencils set? Or, should she take a chance at one that gave no clues, a regular Lucky Dip?

There had also been a section of the Pavilion for animals, and she had been able to feel the soft warm fur of white rabbits and watch the baby chicks dashing around, chirping noisily.

As a young child, the annual Bathurst Show had been a time of new experiences and wonderment for Grace.

As a young woman, the Dubbo Show would prove to be a time of new experiences and wonder on an entirely different level for her.

Grace discovered there was actually much more to do at an annual country town Show than explore Sideshow Alley or the Pavilion, although the Pavilion still held interest for her.

It seemed Rachel and Jess agreed, especially as it had started to drizzle at that moment. The Pavilion would be the ideal place to be while they waited for the Wood-Chopping event. However, Darel and Martin excused themselves from joining the group because they wanted to watch the Sheep-Dog Trials. They said they weren't at all concerned about a little rain. Dan said he wanted to check out some things in the Pavilion, so he was happy to tag along with the girls.

Rachel, Jess, Grace and Dan all enter the Pavilion together, but quickly disperse; Rachel and Jess wandering off to look at the needlework and cooking sections while Grace and Dan veer towards the photography and art.

Soon, oblivious to other people around them, Grace and Dan walk along the lines of paintings in contemplation, comparing their likes and dislikes. Grace pauses at a rural scene depicting a river. She is just about to make a comment about it when a voice she vaguely recognises interrupts her thoughts. She turns and finds Jasmine standing beside Dan.

"Well, hello there Dan," Jasmine half-sings. "Fancy seeing you here? I don't recall you ever coming to the Show before."

"Hello Jasmine," he replies looking over to Grace, giving Jasmine an opportunity to greet her also. She doesn't.

"Now Dan," Jasmine continues, flicking some invisible thread or bug from his arm, but leaving her hand there afterwards, "I hope to see you at home sometime soon. You know Daddy has been expecting you to call around about that project he's working on. Besides, it's been far too long since you came for dinner," she looks at Grace, and emphasises, "like you used to."

Dan removes her hand from his arm and moves a step closer to Grace. He chuckles, suddenly appearing amused. "Jasmine, I did enjoy the lovely meal your mother insisted I stay for the time I was at your home discussing some business with your father. However, it was the one and only time."

"Well, be that as it may Dan, I know you just love my lemon meringue pie. If you are good I might even let you take home the one I entered into the pie section today. It's sure to win." She finally looks over at Grace. "So what have you entered Grace dear?"

Dan interrupts, now beginning to look irritated. "Jasmine, please tell your father I apologise for not getting back to him yet, but I've been quite busy."

"Oh yes, I know how busy you've been Dan Matthews," Jasmine spits out, becoming angry now her tactic obviously hasn't worked. "Cat saw how busy you've been. She was celebrating her one year anniversary with Tom the night you were at the *Quality Inn*."

Dan decides he's had enough of Jasmine's interference. "Jasmine, I'll call your father myself on Monday. In fact, I think it might be better if he comes into Council to see me in future."

"Dan Matthews, you have gone just too far. Don't you realise that you are ruining yourself and *opportunities* by flirting with unknowns?"

Grace opens her mouth to respond, finding it almost impossible to remain quiet now, but Dan intercedes.

"Jasmine, Grace and I are going now. We'll see you at tennis." He takes Grace by the arm, turns and walks away with her. His face is red and he is scowling.

Rachel and Jess suddenly appear beside them.

Rachel notices the look on Dan's face and that Grace is looking rather agitated. "Is everything alright?" she whispers to Grace, when Dan looks away.

Grace begins to shake her head from side-to-side as if to say – no, but stops and gives Rachel a half-smile and says, "Yes, everything is fine. Is it nearly time for the Wood-Chopping event, do you think?"

Dan quickly regains his composure and looks at Grace. "I'm sorry about that," he says quietly.

"It's not your fault. Don't worry, I'm fine," she attempts to reassure him although she is still unsure if she is in fact – *fine*.

He sighs deeply. "I'd better make my way over there now, anyway," he says.

Amidst a chorus of *good luck* and, *we'll be there soon*, he leaves the three woman to talk about what had made him so mad.

After explaining what happened, Grace asks Rachel, "Who's Cat?"

Rachel groans. "Jasmine's side-kick, Catherine Dobermann, Cat for short. I don't know her personally, but I've heard people say she has a reputation for being - *catty*, and her surname suits her well too because she has a way of sniffing out the most interesting gossip. She's very loyal to Jasmine apparently.

"What does she look like?"

"She's fairly short and plump, and she has bleached blond, hair; almost white. Well, that's the colour it was last time I saw her a few months ago."

"I can't remember seeing her that night. Come to think of it, I don't really remember much about anyone who was there; beside Dan," Grace adds, with a glint in her eye that Rachel and Jess can't help but notice.

"Well, that's no surprise," Jess says cheekily.

Rachel adds, "It's hard to miss her, so you must really have been in your own world." She grins then and Grace rolls her eyes, takes her by the arm, and they all walk out of the Pavilion.

They head over to the Wood-Chopping event, to where Dan and Darel will both be competing, skilfully avoiding any large puddles of water or muddy areas on their way.

Grace, Rachel and Jess arrive at the Wood-Chopping event and find Martin. He is looking into a fenced off area, where six men each stand beside a log positioned horizontally in a steel cradle. They are all holding an axe and there are wood shavings already around each log. Martin points to Dan and Darel at the far end of the enclosure. They all walk quickly around the enclosure to be as close as possible to them.

All six men are wearing singlets in different shades and styles, and either work trousers or jeans. Grace looks at Dan's well defined bare muscles and she feels goose bumps suddenly appear on her arms. She giggles, thinking about how astute Mary was about Dan's muscles.

"What?" Rachel asks, hearing her giggle.

"Nothing," she answers.

"I don't know who to go for," Jess says. "Darel or Dan, I mean," she clarifies when Grace and Rachel both look at her. "I guess I'll just have to take it in turns. Actually, that's not a bad idea, because either way, if either of them win, I'll have gone for the winner."

"You've got it all worked out honey, as usual," Martin says, giving her a cuddle from behind.

Darel looks over and spots the group and immediately calls to Dan. Dan then looks where he is pointing and smiles at Grace. She mouths, *good luck*, and then a man begins to speak through a microphone at the side of the enclosure.

"Good afternoon folks. We're almost ready to start the Wood-Chopping event, called, *underhand*. Now before we begin, for all those who have never witnessed any of the different styles, the underhand is considered to be the easiest, although Jack Newman, winner last year and the year before, will tell you it's, 'still harder than it looks'. Now, although Jack likes us to believe that it is, as he says, 'still harder than it looks', because he's won this event two times in a row, we're going to give the newcomers a little head start, in the name of fairness. So, when you hear the hooter go the first time, Jack will be having a little break while the newcomers start. And a minute later the hooter will blow for Jack to start. So, while the rain's holding back for us - are we ready?" he asks, although he is really telling the participants to get ready for the hooter.

All six axemen stand on their blocks with their legs apart, holding their axes with both hands. The hooter sounds and the wood chips start flying, joining the wood chips that were already lying on the ground before they started. While the referee had been commentating, Martin had explained to the women that the earlier woodchips were there because the axemen had already cut out foot holds in readiness for the event.

It was easy to see who Jack Newman was. He was the only one not chopping, and it seemed like the other five men were doing very well for newcomers. They all seemed to be ploughing through their logs at an alarming rate. Then, the hooter sounded and Jack was off. In less than two minutes he had caught up to them, and Grace couldn't help herself when she saw Dan so close to finishing. "C'mon Dan," she yelled. Well, that set Rachel off, and soon the three women were yelling, "C'mon Dan, Go Darel, and, Go Darel and Dan." Even Martin was affected, although he barracked for Darel. Then suddenly, Darel jumped down from the block as his log broke in half, and Dan followed a few seconds later. Jack Newman came next. Dan and Darel's fan team clapped excitedly as the winner was announced and Dan went up to Darel and shook his hand. Jack Newman also shook Darel's hand and then all the axemen collected their shirts and made their way out of the enclosure.

As soon as Darel exits the enclosure, Rachel races up to him, wraps her arms around him and kisses him fully on the mouth.

Grace stands close to Dan and says with her eyes sparkling, "That was so impressive."

"Thanks Grace. I guess your mother would think so too, hey?"

Grace laughs and nods.

Rachel, Darel, Jess and Martin all saunter off, away from the enclosure.

A man walks up to Dan and Grace. "You did good Dan. Shame you had to lose to that bloody abo."

Grace flinches, and Dan's face drops.

He looks at John Mills, someone he knows from working at the Council, and replies with a deadpanned look, "Yeah well, Darel takes after his father, Don Rutherford, who won this same event many times in his younger days. Darel deserved to win; too good for me John." He takes Grace by the hand and turns to leave, but turns back momentarily. "And by the way, he's a friend of mine," he adds firmly.

Grace is in shock, she's never heard anyone refer to anyone like that before. And it wasn't so much as what he said, but the *way* he said it; with such distaste, almost disgust. She reasons that she may be a bit naïve in that respect, knowing that she was pretty much protected from many things through having white parents and looking white. But, it not only hurt to hear obvious racism, but also someone saying that about her brother, and someone who looked as white as his father. Grace wonders if other people have said anything like that to Dan about her. All of a sudden, she feels a little paranoid. Were people talking about her like that too?

Dan stops walking and Grace follows suit automatically. He moves in front of her, to face her fully. He can clearly see she has been shaken by what John Mills said. As if knowing her thoughts, he places his hands on her shoulders and looks into her eyes, "It's wrong Grace, but just in case you're wondering, if anyone ever says anything like that to me again about anyone in your family, I will remind them of what wonderful people the Rutherfords are, and I will also tell them…well, you don't really need to know what I might say, *if* there's a next time."

Grace nods, still taking in his words. She is somewhat reassured, but wonders if he will always feel that way.

"Is there anything else you'd like to do or see here, or would you like to go?"

"No, I think I'd like to go, thanks. Besides, we're all going out to dinner at the Club tonight, remember?"

# CHAPTER 8

The busiest times of the year for the Dubbo Services Club were commonly the days marked on the calendar for, The Melbourne Cup, the Picnic Races, and the Show weekend. As many people converged on the town during those times, socialising at the Club was a regular occurrence. The Pubs always did a roaring trade in the tradition of liquid celebration, and the town's restaurants satisfied those looking for a refined, celebratory, dining experience. But, it was the Club which drew the masses; a place which catered for both young and old, in search of a place to both eat and drink in a relaxed atmosphere.

On those particular times of the year, the Club buzzed with activity. In the bar, lounge, dance and poker machine areas, people would need to manoeuver through the crowds, side-stepping each other, or lean in close to hear a companion's remarks over the hum of voices or loud music. At least, in the Bistro area, cocooned in a separate room, there would be some reprieve for tired legs and ringing ears. Once seated, apart from being summoned to collect an ordered meal, diners could relax in their seats and enjoy each other's company.

Between the time Dan had dropped her off at the flat after the Show, and when he had picked her up to go to the Club, Grace had been unable to stop thinking about what had happened earlier. Yes, it was true that two incidences at the Show had offended her; first Jasmine's words about her to Dan, and then that man's words about Darel. On both occasions, Dan had intervened and stood up for her, and Darel. She had been impressed by the way he had kept his cool, although his reddened face and scowl on both occasions had reflected an internal battle. But he had shown where his loyalty lay. In Darel's case, it could have been more understandable, given that he had obviously known him for many years. In her case, however, it just proved that he already had strong feelings for her.

His passion for his work was obvious, and she had seen first-hand how his position at the Council meant that his work life often spilled over to, or was in actuality, part and parcel of his personal life. She could easily see he would continue to do well at work and had no doubt that he would one day hold a prominent position within Council. He knew how to remain polite and professional, even when placed in confronting situations. She can't imagine he had learnt how to do that through his work. It had to be just the way he was, a gentleman. Yes, she may have been offended earlier, but on both occasions Dan had shown, he had-her-back. She really shouldn't worry.

They had managed to secure a table for eight, which had been no small feat at the Club that night. Though Johno turned up alone and could easily have felt a little left out among the three sets of couples, especially now his elder brother was dating Grace, he didn't seem all that concerned. However, she soon found out why, when Rachel updated her in the ladies room.

"I forgot to tell you about Johno. He's got his eye on a new girl at work. He told me last Wednesday at tennis while you were talking to Dan. She started two weeks ago, and he's not sure whether he should ask her out or not. He doesn't want to upset his father."

"Why would it upset his father?"

"Well, he dated the last office admin they had there, and she left soon after their second date. He said his father will kill him if the same thing happens with the new girl."

"But surely he can't blame Johno for the first girl leaving. It probably had nothing to do with their dates."

"Yeah, well anyway, he said he's trying not to make the first move. At least that way if it doesn't go anywhere, or if she quits her job, he can tell his father that *she* pursued *him*. But, he reckons it probably wouldn't make much difference in the long run. He said his father would still kill him."

Grace chuckled as Rachel smiled. "Poor Johno. Well, I hope she's a nice girl, because he deserves a nice girl."

"Yep!" Rachel had replied as they put away their lipstick and headed back out to their table.

It seemed the day out at the Show had given them all good appetites, because every one of the group ate with relish once their food arrived. Johno always had a good appetite though, and did justice to any food. He looked at both Dan and Darel, between mouthfuls, and apologised for not being there to cheer them on in the Wood-Chopping event. He said the new girl at the office had told him yesterday that she was having car trouble, but he had been flat-out all day and hadn't had a chance to look at her car by knocking off time the previous day. But, he hadn't wanted to leave her in the lurch, so he'd told her he'd have a look at it in the morning, even though it was Saturday. He figured he'd have plenty of time to make it to the Wood-Chopping event in the afternoon. However, she had run late, and he hadn't realised he had missed the event until after she had driven off from the work-shop.

"Well, you have to look after the staff, you know," he said seriously, placing his knife and fork together onto his plate. Rachel and Grace had shared a private grin.

Jess and Martin decided to have a gamble on the pokies then, having finished their meals. Johno joined them. Rachel noticed music had just started up in the room next to the Bistro. "Who's playing tonight? Do you know?" She looks at Darel. He shakes his head.

They all remain quiet, listening.

"It's not a band. It sounds like a DJ," Dan decides.

Rachel looks at Darel, Grace and Dan in turn. "Let's go have a look. Yeah?" she asks.

They all move from the Bistro, and manage to grab four seats and a table, suddenly vacant, in the dancing area next door. The local DJ had set up on the stage and almost half the dance floor was already filled with people jumping around to, 'In The Summertime' by the Mixtures.

Darel offers to buy a round of drinks and goes off to the bar. Grace can't help herself and starts dancing in her seat. This is the cue Dan needs. He stands and holds out his hand to Grace, and she takes it joyfully. By the time Darel returns with their drinks, Dan and Grace are dancing apart on the dancefloor and looking at each other with huge smiles. The song ends and Grace looks up to where Rachel and Darel are sitting. She notices they have moved their seats closer together and Rachel is snuggled against Darel, but she spots Grace looking and smiles and waves. Grace can see she isn't in any hurry to come onto the dance floor yet. They all know that if they all leave the table at the same time they could lose it. Dan doesn't seem in any hurry to leave the dance floor anyway. They both look towards the stage, waiting to see what the next song will be. When the recent 'YMCA' by the Village People starts, they both resume their dancing, although the dance floor is almost completely full now. They move closer together. After the song finishes, Grace indicates that she needs a drink, so they head back to the table. Then Darel gently disengages from Rachel and takes her hand, pulling her up to the dance floor for the next few songs.

They are all at the table a little later when the DJ puts on, 'Lay Your Love On Me' by Racey. Dan is up in a flash looking down at Grace with the unspoken question. As he walks onto the dance floor this time though, instead of releasing her hand, he pulls her close and they move as one to the song. He looks into her eyes and starts to sing along with the lyrics. *When I first saw you, baby I knew, ooh darling it had to be you, you're the one who takes me high-er, ooh baby set my heart on fire. Come on baby lay your love on me, ooh baby let your love go free now, come on baby lay your love on me, baby, baby, baby, you've got the love I need now'.* Grace feels like she is floating. It is one of the happiest moments of her life. She has this amazing man staring into her eyes, asking her to love him. At the end of the song, he is still holding her close. He leans down and whispers in her ear. "Would you like to go and look at the full moon? The rain is supposed to have eased up, so we could go and sit by the river for a while, if you like."

"Well, that sounds nice. Yes, lets! I just need to go to the ladies first though."

Dan said he would wait for her back at the table. She heads to the ladies room.

Oblivious to anything happening around them, from the moment they had entered the dance room, Grace, Dan, Rachel and Darel had been unaware that three women had been watching the couples intently. Hidden in the corner from view, camouflaged by the throngs of people moving around, Jasmine Healy, Catherine Dobermann and Leanne Cooper, sat observing the couples, and in particular Grace and Dan on the dance floor.

Jasmine Healy has known Dan all her life. They had been in the same class at school. Even as a child she had been attracted to him, and more and more as he grew into adolescence. He had never responded to her feeble attempts to gain his attention then, however, so she had eventually given up trying; instead, manufacturing faults in her mind that deemed him unworthy of her efforts.

By the time he started work at the Council though, she couldn't ignore the fact that those same failings she had held previously in her mind, had somehow mysteriously, disappeared. And besides, her father admired him. Therefore, if she were to succeed in winning Dan's affections, her father would be proud of her, and no doubt reward her handsomely. He had been quick to punish her for her previous misadventures, and although no-one would be any the wiser, she had known full well the brunt of his displeasure. Hadn't the Hunter boy's parents widely voiced their opposition to his plans for the new development in their residential area? Jasmine had been quick to respond that Ray Hunter had not said anything himself.

"Ahh, that's true Jazzie, as he affectionately called her, *but* the fruit never falls far from the tree. You had better remember that, and if you want to live in the same style as your mother, even after you marry, then you had better choose well."

Since that conversation with her father, it had become Jasmine's mission to seduce Dan. She had placed herself in numerous situations to implement her plan; at the gym, tennis, the cricket, and even by calling into the Council to ask him questions about the development planning process, although it bored her nearly to tears. She figured it was as good an excuse as any to talk to him, and would seem feasible under the circumstance. Her father had been pleased to see Jasmine's interest in Daniel Matthews. He had even assisted her by asking Dan to call around to his home, and kept Dan talking long enough for his wife to insist he stay for dinner.

Jasmine had walked Dan out to his car after dinner that night. She couldn't have wished for a better opportunity. At the second step down from the verandah, she accidentally slipped. Dan had reached across and held on to her to prevent her from falling. She had then reached up and placed her arms around his neck, pressing her body closely against him. He had begun to speak, but she had silenced him by planting her lips firmly upon his. She had enjoyed feeling his firm chest against her breasts, and his lips under hers. But, she hadn't enjoyed his response. He had resisted, pushing her gently away as he ensured she stood steady on the step. She had been shocked by his response, never before being rejected. She had been speechless.

"Thank you for dinner Jasmine," he had said, and walked briskly down the steps and left, without a backward glance.

She had never been so embarrassed, or livid. No-one rejects Jasmine Healy; how dare *he*! However, later on when she had calmed down a little, she attempted to rationalise his actions. Perhaps he had been taken by surprise. He was so manly, of course he would want to make the first move. Next time she would plan it better. But then Grace had appeared.

Catherine Dobermann, known locally as Cat, and Leanne Cooper, had been Jasmine Healy's followers for as long as they could remember. Although they both considered themselves Jasmine's closest friends, they had long ago come to accept that the friendship didn't exist without condition. Any gossip circulating was to be brought to Jasmine's notice, as quickly as possible, and they had better be prepared to do what was necessary to allow Jasmine to proceed with whatever plan she had in place at the time. Their reward was that they could be publicly known as her friends, with the added benefit of being associated with the wealthier class of Dubbo.

Cat and Leanne had been subjected to Jasmine's whining about Grace Taylor all evening. But Cat glowed with pride. She had informed Jasmine the very next morning, after noticing Grace and Dan flirting at the restaurant that night. She had not held back in details; the way they had looked at each other across the candlelit table, fed food to each other, and even how Dan had kissed Grace's fingertips. Yes, Jasmine had been more than interested in the information she had relayed.

Leanne, on the other hand, was feeling the pressure. She hadn't had anything to add about Grace, even though she had kept her ear open for even the slightest hint of information wherever she went. Leanne listened to Jasmine's festering displeasure of this newcomer to the district, and racked her brain trying to think of anyone who might know something she could use against her. Having nothing to add to the discussion, Leanne decided to replenish their drinks at the bar. At least that was something she could do in an attempt to stay in Jasmine's good books.

A short while later, she was standing at the bar, watching the bartender fill her order, when she happened to overhear a conversation between two men close by.

"Yeah, can't fault Dan though," one of the men said as he leaned against the bar with a beer in his hand.

"Naw, he's a good bloke. Besides, you don't want ta get on the wrong side of anyone working at Council," the other man offered.

"Yeah! But, so what if I called the Rutherford boy an abo?" the first man adds. "It's true, ain't it?"

"Yeah, everyone knows Don Rutherford married that half-caste after his missus died," the second man confirms.

"So, technically, that son of theirs is also part abo, or quarter, or whatever ya wanna call it. Still – abo."

"Yep!" His companion again confirms.

Leanne can't believe her luck. She even comes close to thanking the heavens for seeing her plight and blessing her. She quickly paid for the drinks and heads back to her table.

"Well, well, well," Jasmine sneers, after hearing the news. "Now, isn't that interesting," she says, twirling the straw in her vodka and orange, thinking. "Sooo, if Darel is part aborigine and Grace is his sister, as she told me at tennis, it stands to reason, she's also part aborigine," Jasmine finally says with a look of glee on her face.

Jasmine them tosses ideas back and forth to her two companions as she catches glimpses of Grace and Dan on the dance floor through the crowd. She had made another attempt with Dan at the Show earlier today. It hadn't gone well at all, because of Grace. It seems the only way she was going to get anywhere with Dan is to get Grace out of the picture. An idea forms…

"Do you remember that guy who worked at that real estate place? The one who married that half-caste? she asks Cat and Leanne.

"Yeah, Mark something," Cat says eagerly.

"Hmm, I have an idea," Jasmine says smugly.

The three heads come closer together towards the middle of the table.

Grace makes her way into the ladies room. It's completely vacant. She walks to the toilet stall at the far end and closes the door. The door to the ladies room opens, and two sets of high heels tap their way to the wash basins. Grace can hear zippers opening. She assumes they are probably attending to their make-up. She is just about to flush the toilet when one of the women asks her companion a question, causing Grace to pause.

"Hey, did you hear what they're saying about Dan Matthews?"

"You mean about that woman he's with now being part abo? the second woman responds.

"Yep, the word is - he's too good for the likes of her."

Lips smack together and lipstick lids are put back on.

"Hmm, it's such a shame," the second woman adds. "She'll probably ruin his chance in the community now. It happened to Mark at Elders Real Estate when he married that half-caste. He never did well after that, even though he was one of their best sales people."

The first woman continues, "Yeah, and his kids ended up spending more time with his wife's family than his and getting into trouble at school." She concludes, "Anyway, I doubt she'll be with Dan much longer though. He'll come to his senses and get over his tiff with Jasmine. And, he'll end up a Councillor, especially if Jasmine's father has anything to do with it."

"Yeah, no doubt there," the second woman responds.

And then the two women leave the ladies room.

Jasmine mechanically flushes the toilet and walks out of the cubicle. She's walks over to the wash basins.

A few minutes later, the noise from the ladies room door opening causes her to snap out of the trance-like state she has been in. She flinches momentarily as Rachel walks in.

"Hey Grace," Rachel says with a smile, that instantly drops the moment she looks closer at Grace's face. "Are you ok?" she now asks, starting to frown.

Grace looks at Rachel in the reflection of the mirror. She has been standing here at the wash basins, staring at herself in the mirror, ever since the two women left. If it weren't for all the wonderful moments she has experienced today and tonight, she would be nearly convinced she were in a bad dream. And Rachel has just woken her.

She turns and looks at Rachel face-to-face. She can see she is starting to look worried. She doesn't want to spoil her night by sharing what she had heard. Besides, she's not sure she wants to tell her anyway. Snap out of it Grace, she admonishes herself.

"Yes, I'm fine. Sorry, I guess I was just off with the fairies for a while there."

Rachel sighs in relief and her frown changes into a grin. "Oh good. Dan sent me in here to see if you were alright. Can you believe it?"

Grace manages to chuckle softly. "I guess he wants to get going."

"Yeah, he told us you were going. Are you going back to our place?"

"No, he wants to take me to look at the full moon, by the river," she replies, looking very self-satisfied.

"Ohhh, way to go Grace. Don't do anything I wouldn't do," Rachel replies grinning.

"Well, I'm not sure that leaves me with much, not to do," she counters, rolling her eyes.

"Oi, sister-in-law to-be, you're talking to a soon-to-be married person here. It's pretty much a given," Rachel says with a cheeky grin as they walk out of the ladies room.

Rachel has lifted her spirits and she tries to completely forget about what those two women said. However, as she is walking with Rachel towards Dan and Darel at the table, she suddenly feels as if she is being watched, and she wonders if those two women are still around.

As Dan and Grace make their way out of the club, Grace looks tentatively around at the crowd of people, glancing quickly at faces, and also in corners. She pulls up abruptly when she spots three women in a far corner, all looking at her. And she notices Jasmine. All three of them immediately look away. *Hmmm*, she wonders. *What a coincidence.* She looks at Dan and notices he is turning to see where she is looking, but she doesn't want him to see Jasmine, so she claims his attention.

"Sorry, I just thought I recognised someone. I must have been mistaken."

Dan nods, takes her by the hand and they walk out of the Club.

# CHAPTER 9

Dan pulls up at Sandy Beach Park, as close to the river as the edge of the car parking area will allow. He gets out of the Jeep and walks around to assist Grace to climb down the passenger side. He opens the back passenger side door and reaches in and pulls out a dark blue, yellow striped, picnic blanket.

"The grass might still be wet," he says, explaining why he has grabbed the picnic blanket.

"Good idea," she responds. "I guess the rain is good for the countryside, but we've sure had a lot this week." She has a thought, "What happens if the tennis courts get too wet?"

They step through the gap between the pine logs which border the car parking area.

"Hmm, I think it just gets postponed until they dry out. Yes, I remember that happening before." He turns to her, and his face lights up. "We'll just have to find something else to do on a Wednesday night if that's the case." He waits for her confirmation.

Grace smiles. "Yes, guess so."

So far, she's felt grateful knowing she will see him at least every Wednesday night, and now she's reassured he's had a similar thought. They walk over to a grassy spot overlooking the river. Dan spreads the blanket. They are both soon gazing up at the moon, their arms wrapped around their bended knees.

Grace sighs. "I'm so glad we can see it. It's beautiful, isn't it?"

"It sure is." He pauses for a moment. "And so are you Grace," he says, his voice drawing her eyes to his face.

"Thank you Dan," she replies softly.

He doesn't attempt to move any closer, nor reach out to her. It is something she is not used to. Any of the men she had previously been with would have taken the opportunity. Strangely, she finds his complimentary words so much more meaningful, sincere, this way.

He turns to look ahead and she follows his gaze to the water, bathed in the glorious glow of the full moon. They both become mesmerized by its beauty and momentarily lost in their private thoughts.

Grace wishes she could think back on this day, only with joy. She will never forget the moments she has spent with Dan, earlier at the Show, and just recently at the Club.

She had enjoyed walking around the Pavilion by his side, looking at the products and produce of local businesses, as they made their way to the art and photography sections. She had been fascinated to discover his taste in art to be more abstract then she would have thought, although she was pleased to see he was also very fond of nature scenes. She would never forget watching him in the Wood Chopping event, though she hoped no-one had observed her studying every part of him as his muscles worked overtime on the log. Then tonight, as they danced, he had held her in his arms and sung to her.

And right now, they were sitting side-by-side beside a tranquil river underneath a glorious full moon. She has every reason to feel this to be one of the happiest days of her life.

John Mills, Jasmine Healy and those two women had tried to spoil it for her though. And they had come very close to succeeding. Things happen in threes, they say. Well, at least there shouldn't be any more shocks today. Yes, she had been shocked, by all three incidences. Yet, although she doesn't feel as vulnerable now, she is still hurting from the experiences.

It appears she is going to have to toughen up. After what those two women had said, it's now obvious John Mills isn't the only person in the community with racist views. She tries to just look at the stupidity of it. They weren't even judging her and Darel because of their skin-colour. It was because their mother had honey coloured skin. Racism was so ridiculous. But knowing that still didn't change the fact . that there would always be people with those attitudes. She suddenly realises Darel hasn't said anything to her about any problems he's had. She'd be amazed if he's managed to remain unscathed all his life, judging by what happened today. Perhaps she should ask him how he handled it. After all, sooner or later more people were going to find out she was his sister.

As for Jasmine, well, Dan had told her that she was nothing more than a friend, although after the Pavilion incident she had wondered if he felt he could even call her that. However, he had also said at one point that he owed her father a lot, helping him when he first started at the Council. She imagines that would put him in a bit of a predicament;

knowing how dedicated he was to his work.

Could those two women be right about Dan and Jasmine though? From the way they had talked it sounded like they were locals, and she was fast becoming aware that the locals knew a great deal more than even she thought. Dan had said Jasmine was no more than a friend, but that was – now. Had they ever been close in the past? Sometimes news takes time to get around. Perhaps the tiff between Dan and Jasmine they referred to had happened a while ago. It was possible.

And then there was the way those two women had talked about her not being good enough for Dan. She had felt like such a coward, remaining in the toilet cubicle until they left. She should have gone out and told them to mind their own business; stuck up for herself. But, what would she have said? Could she have denied their words? What would have been the point in letting them know that she had heard them state, what could be for all she knew - fact?

What they had said, however, about her involvement with Dan ruining his reputation was something she didn't want to think about right now. She sighs deeply.

"That's a big sigh. Is everything alright?" Dan asks, once more turning to her.

"Ahum, just thinking about today."

"Ok, so what's the consensus?"

She moves closer to him and takes his hand. "Well, I have to say, without doubt, it's been a day I will always remember."

"Hmm, I hope that's because of the good parts," he asks, looking at her intently, and rubbing his thumb gently over her hand.

She looks into his eyes, and she can see he is waiting expectantly, and hoping - hoping that all he has done for her today has made up for those difficult moments. She moves even closer to him, and reaches out with her free hand to touch his cheek. "Yes, and - thank you," she says softly.

He leans toward her, their lips meet, and at that moment nothing else matters.

# CHAPTER 10

If it hadn't been for the mosquitoes attacking Grace and Dan at the river, they would have stayed there much longer, but even so, by the time Dan pulled up at her flat, it was shrouded in darkness. Rachel, Jess and Darel had no doubt been asleep for quite a while. He had helped her to step down from the Jeep, held her in his arms again and kissed her goodnight. He had then watched her make her way up the stairs and walk quietly inside. She had heard him start the Jeep and drive off, then fallen into bed a few minutes later, drifting off quickly into a deep slumber.

On Sunday morning, Grace walked into the lounge room to find Rachel and Jess discussing the wedding, with Darel watching them with a contented smile. Rachel had asked Jess to be her bridesmaid on Friday night, soon after she had arrived. Grace had not needed to worry about Jess taking offence at not being asked to be Maid of Honour. She had been beside herself with joy at the news of the wedding and even told Grace on the side that she was relieved knowing she would be there to help Rachel prepare for it.

As Darel was leaving to go back to Binda, he reminded Grace that their mother was expecting her at Jannali the following Friday night. He said he's been given strict instructions to make sure he told her, even though he knew she wouldn't let their mother down. He then jokingly reminded Rachel that he expected to see her on Saturday, in case she forgot.

"Oh get going", Rachel had told him, feigning annoyance, "As if I would forget."

They then both spent another ten minutes talking about how much they missed each other, and kissing and cuddling. Grace had discretely left the room to start on the laundry which hadn't been done the day before because of the Show. Jess had headed for the bathroom to collect her toiletry bag and anything else she had brought with her that wasn't already in her overnight bag.

Darel finally left after saying he would see them both on Wednesday night at tennis, and Jess followed quickly after him, to collect Martin from Johno's flat and return to Canberra.

Grace and Rachel did a quick tidy-up of the flat, and then decided they deserved to put their feet up for a while. Besides it had started raining heavily again, so they couldn't do much else.

Rachel suggested they watch a video, and that reminded Grace of a new movie she'd heard about at work. The movie was called, Alien, and she'd been told that Sigourney Weaver was really good. So they jumped into Grace's Corolla and headed down to Video Ezy to hire the movie. They had just arrived back and had settled down on the lounge ready to press 'play' on the VCR when there was a knock on the door. Grace went to answer it, and opened the door to see Dan.

"Oh, good afternoon," she said with a huge smile, mirroring his.

"Hello beautiful. I was just passing by, no – I wasn't really; that's a lie. I was wondering if you'd like to do something this arvo, if you're not busy. You know, it would be a great deal easier if you had a telephone so I could pester you that way. And that way at least I wouldn't put you on the spot like this."

Grace's smile hasn't changed since she opened the door. She has found his slight embarrassment, very endearing. "Why don't you come in," she says, taking his hand and pulling him inside.

"Hi Dan," Rachel says from the lounge which is adjacent to the front door.

"Hi Rachel." He notices she has a video case beside her. "Well, it looks like I'm interrupting," he says.

"No, that's ok." Rachel says and looks to Grace.

Grace doesn't want to desert Rachel. She enjoys watching movies with her too. But if Dan wants her to go somewhere with him she will, at the drop of a hat. Maybe she can do both at the same time.

"Dan, have you seen Alien, yet?" she asks.

"No, is that the new one out?" he asks, looking interested.

"Yep. Would you like to watch it with us? Is that ok with you Rachel?"

"Yeah, of course. You know, it's going to be quite scary. I've just read the cover properly," Rachel says, biting her bottom lip.

"Well, it sounds like we had better watch it together," Dan says, making a pretence of seriousness.

So, they watched the movie together, and Rachel only screamed once, while Grace hid her face against Dan's chest, several times. Grace had thoroughly enjoyed being snuggled up on the lounge with Dan.

Rachel had opted to sit in the bean bag closer to the screen and Grace knew she had done that to give her and Dan a bit of privacy behind her.

After the movie, Dan offered to drop the movie back at the video shop on his way home. He said he really should go. He had been putting off some odd jobs that needed doing. He held Grace close and thanked her for inviting him to watch the movie with them. He asked her if she would like to do the same at his place sometime. He said he'd like to show her where he lives. She said she'd like that, perhaps the weekend following the next.

"Of course," he said. "Your mother is expecting you at Jannali next weekend."

"Yes, even *you* can't keep me away from her then."

"I understand. Besides, I'd hate to be the cause of upsetting your mother," he'd replied. Then he had looked deep into her eyes and kissed her. "I'll see you Wednesday night, at tennis then, if not before."

She then watched him drive away, and humming the song he had sung to her at the Club, danced up the steps to the flat.

# CHAPTER 11

It had been a busy start to the week at the Dubbo Medical Centre. Grace had found herself answering non-stop calls from people wanting to make appointments. It was as if the spring weather had suddenly brought on an allergy epidemic. Or perhaps all the rain had stirred these ailments up.

There were mothers bringing in small children with swollen red eyes, teenagers scratching non-stop and elderly people coughing and wheezing. That was on top of the usual scheduled appointments. She was so glad she wasn't prone to these quite common seasonal ailments.

Then there had been the problem with the fax machine *and* the printer, as well as being one employee short, who had called in sick as soon as she had walked into the centre Monday morning. She had found herself juggling several duties which were not normally hers, as well as her own. So, by the time Wednesday came around, she was looking forward to seeing Dan at tennis.

But, she didn't see him at tennis that night. The Wednesday night tennis comp was postponed, due to the rain. The consensus was that the Dubbo area had received more rain in the last month than they had in the preceding six months, which also included the normal rainfall for winter.

However, as Dan had suggested, they found other things to do while the rain had its way, and they waited for the courts to dry. Instead of going to tennis that Wednesday night, he had taken her ten-pin bowling.

The last time she had played had been at Bathurst, with a couple of her work friends. She had quite enjoyed ten-pin bowling at Bathurst, but with Dan it was more fun than she could have ever imagined ten-pin bowling could be. She was convinced he deliberately played badly, although he was adamant he had never played well.

"Why did you suggest we come then," she had asked as he was mid-way in bowling a ball "if you knew you were going to embarrass yourself," she had giggled. He had then lost concentration, let go of the ball and with a disgusted look, watched it fall into the gutter.

"Well," he had then said, feigning seriousness, "I'm not one to show off, or hadn't you noticed?" But, he had then lost the ability to pretend any longer, and grinning mischievously, pounced on her and pulled her close. "Besides, I love seeing you having fun, instead of worrying about winning like you do at tennis. You make me happy when you're happy," he had said softly, bending forward to kiss her gently on the lips.

Although Grace enjoyed playing tennis with her friends, it couldn't compare to her time alone with Dan. And although she hadn't been able to completely forget about the incidences at the Show and Club, she decided she wasn't going to entertain her previous concerns about her relationship with Dan anymore. As far as she was concerned that was all behind her now. Life was so very good at the moment, and she wasn't about to let anything spoil it.

She found herself daydreaming quite often these days, which didn't help her concentration at work, especially when they had been as busy as they had recently. In a way, it reminded her of how the same thing had happened at work in Bathurst, when she had been consumed with thoughts about meeting her mother for the first time. This time, however, when her co-workers looked at her with raised eyebrows and grins, she knew they had it right; her lack of concentration was because of a man. And this time, she didn't look tired from tossing and turning in her bed, her mind whirling from anticipation and unanswered questions. This time she was well rested, going to sleep each night with a smile on her face, greeting each new day with a new spring in her step, and eyes that sparkled with joy.

Dan had picked her up from the flat virtually straight after work, that Wednesday evening, so by the time they finished at the ten-pin bowling alley, both their stomachs were growling for food.

"I think we better eat, by the sounds of that" he said with a grin, as Grace blushed with embarrassment at the noises emitting from her stomach. "Do you like Chinese?"

"Yes, that sounds great," she answered, hoping her stomach would now keep quiet, knowing food was on its way.

Dan looks at her thoughtfully. "Would you like to get take-away? You haven't been to my house yet. I'd like you to see it."

"Yes, I'd like that," she said, now more curious than ever.

"Of course, it's not at all grand or unique, like Jannali, but I'd like you to see it all the same."

As he had said, his house wasn't in any way grand. It was a typical medium sized, brick-veneer house, but it was the most modern house she had ever set foot in. She found it had distinct personality too, so to her mind it was definitely, unique.

She had only ever lived in older homes, from the house of her childhood and Binda, both built in the fifties, to the more modern but still dated, flats, in Bathurst and Dubbo. Jannali, of course, was the oldest of them all, but it was a special exception.

Dan watched her reaction closely as they pulled up in the driveway and alighted from the Jeep.

From the driveway, dark coloured tile steps led up to the matching patio, enclosed by an ornate, white, caste iron railing and matching table and chairs. Grace admired the thriving potted shrubs situated in each corner of the patio, and beside the front door.

"The rain is keeping them healthy," he replied to her praise, although Grace didn't believe for a moment they could be so healthy from only recent rain. He obviously had a green thumb.

The front door opened up into a hallway of fresh crème coloured walls lined with several doors to the left, and open sliding glass doors to the right. She followed him as he made his way through the open sliding glass doors, the lounge room, and around to the dining room and kitchen, noting they all had matching neutral coloured painted walls. The kitchen was far more modern than she expected.

Dan explained, as he gave her a tour of the remainder of the house, that he had had the kitchen and bathrooms renovated, and had painted the interior walls of the house himself. He said he remembered now that that had been one reason he hadn't played in the tennis comp the previous year. He had been busy painting and fixing up the house when he hadn't been working.

Three bedrooms, one of which had been turned into an office, and a bathroom, led off from the other end of the hallway from where they had entered the house. Grace was surprised to see the main bedroom also had an ensuite. That was something she had never seen before.

The floors throughout the house were covered by think dark green carpet with a lighter shade of green in a zigzag design. The kitchen floor was covered by sunflower yellow, circular patterned linoleum, and both bathrooms also had matching sunflower dominant colours in the tiles, which lined their floors and the bottom half of the walls. The cupboards and benches of the kitchen and the fittings in the bathrooms were also a cheery sunflower yellow.

"Yellow is my favourite colour, and sunflowers are my favourite flowers," she had explained, when she had seen him notice how her face had lit up when she had first entered the kitchen.

"Ahhh, good to know," he had said with a satisfied look on his face.

The home itself was relatively sparsely furnished, but Grace found that it enhanced rather than detracted from the homely feel of it. Too much clutter often left her feeling uncomfortable. Dan had watched her reaction closely as he led her through his home and he had not been disappointed. It was clear she was both impressed about the house in general and liked the choices he had made.

There were so many new things to discover about Dan, and being giddy with joy at the early stages of new love, Grace had paid little attention to the rain, which had caused the tennis comp matches to be postponed that week.

In fact, the rain had caused her little concern at all, other than to make her ensure she had an umbrella in the car within easy reach, and she hardly noticed the overflowing gutters and waterfalls from rooftops as she drove to work and back home again.

Therefore, it wasn't until she found out that she wouldn't be able to drive out to Jannali that weekend as she had promised her mother that she began to see the seriousness of it all. Mogiguy Creek had overflowed half way between Dubbo and Jannali, covering the Mogiguy bridge on the Newell Highway.

They had almost finished their Chinese take-away, and Grace was still laughing at her fumbled efforts with chopsticks, when they heard about it on the radio.

"Oh, can I…" she began.

"Yes, of course, it's over there," he said, pointing towards the side table along the wall between the kitchen and dining room.

"Mum, are you all ok out there?" she asked anxiously when Mary picked up at her end of the telephone line.

"Yes, daughter, we all good, even Darel. There's no need to worry. The river is doin' just fine here. She a big river, she can take a lot of water."

"I don't know if the water will be down in time for me to come out this weekend as planned. They said on the radio it could take about a week to subside."

"Yeah, I know daughter. I sad about that too, but it ok. It can't be helped. But, you come as soon as it safe to pass over the bridge, ok?

"Yes, of course Mum. I'll let you know as soon as I know I can come. Oh, are you alright for supplies? Do you have enough food for another week?"

"Yeah, don't worry Grace darlin'. We got enough supplies for a month or more. Besides, we could always go fishin' if we hungry," she had said with a giggle.

Grace had missed Marys attempt at humour because Dan was motioning to her, in an attempt to get her attention. "Ok, but, …hang on a tic."

Dan is now standing beside Grace. "Tell your mother that if she wants to contact you at all, any time outside of work hours, she can always call me here and I'll make sure you get the message."

"Did you hear that Mum?" Grace asks down the line.

"Yeah, I did. Dan a real good fella. Tell him that good to know an' thanks. So, best give me the number then."

Grace relayed her mother's message to Dan and Dan repeated his phone number to Grace to pass on to her.

Grace hadn't seen Rachel since they'd both left for work that morning. She had decided that Rachel must have been held up at work because she still hadn't arrived back at the flat by the time Dan had picked her up earlier. Grace asked Mary if she knew if Rachel knew about the bridge. Had she been in touch with Darel?

Mary said Rachel had found out earlier that day, from one of their regular customers at the Store, who had family on the Barwon side. She said Rachel had called her straight after trying Darel's number. She had hoped to catch him at the house even though she knew it was unlikely he would be near it during the day. Mary said she had wanted to get a message to him before he tried to come into town.

Mary added that it was a good thing she was home near a phone most of the time. Darel had been planning on going in to see Rachel that night too, even though there wasn't any tennis on. He wasn't very happy when he heard about the creek, Mary said. Grace imagined Rachel wouldn't be either. But, although she felt sorry for Rachel and Darel, and bad about having to postpone her long weekend at Jannali, once she knew her family were safe, she began to relax again.

When she had finished her conversation with her mother on the phone, Dan decided a diversion was in order, and he said he'd like to show her something out the back.

She followed him through the laundry which led outside to a similar patio to the front of the house, although this area was undercover. A barbeque was positioned to the right, beside an octagonal shaped wooden table, and four two-seater matching wooden chairs.

"Do you entertain much?" she asked looking at the barbeque.

"No, not really. I've only had this place just over a year and I've only just recently finished all I want to do, for now." He hesitates, then adds, "Really though, I prefer to keep things quiet at home. It's kind of like my retreat from everything, if you know what I mean."

Grace could easily see that Dan spent most of his free time fixing up his home. It showed, everywhere she looked.

"You're such a hard worker, and yes, I do know what you mean," she says sincerely.

He smiles at her praise. "Well, if you want something bad enough, you'll put in the effort." His smile changes to a cheeky grin. "Speaking of which, Miss Taylor, I hope you're finding I'm putting in enough effort, where you're concerned."

Grace is caught off guard, but she finally finds her voice. "Yes, well of course, I'm here aren't I? That's all I want Dan; to be able to spend time with you," she adds, and blushes slightly.

Dan takes her hand and pulls it up to his lips and kisses her fingers softly. He then looks out towards a small building to the side, which stands in front of the drive way they had earlier parked in.

"Would you like to see the garage?" he asks. When he doesn't see any instant interest, he adds, "Yes, I use it for storage mostly, but there are other things in there too."

They walk down the steps to the walkway leading to the garage, pausing for a few moments while Grace comments on the fruit trees adorning the outer fence. Dan then points to a small garden section towards the back of the garage. He said he hadn't had time to sort it out yet, but he was looking forward to growing some of his own vegetables, when he got around to it. He was a bit like a hobby farmer in that respect, he added.

Inside the garage, Grace was surprised, yet again, to see so much orderliness. A long work table stood positioned against the opposite wall to the side-door from where they had entered. It was massive and took up almost three-quarters of the length of the wall.

Cupboards and boxes were positioned against the remaining walls, but her attention was drawn back to where Dan was standing.

"I thought I could smell wood shavings," she said brightly, as she looked at the floor. It reminded her of the Wood Chopping event at the Show, and she avoided his eyes at that moment, not wanting to give away her private thoughts.

"Yeah, isn't the smell great?" he says, bringing her back to the moment, and his eyes.

"Sure is. So, what are you up to here," she asks looking curiously at a small cupboard lying on top of a pair of tarp covered saw horses.

"Well, I've just finished sanding it down, so the next job is to put an undercoat on it and then paint it." He looks at her, thinking. "How are your painting skills?" he asks with raised eyebrows.

"Are you serious?" she asks, and he nods. "Well, I wouldn't know," she answers honestly.

"Well, there's one way to find out, I guess," he says with conviction.

So, the following Saturday afternoon, as planned, she arrived at Dan's and he led her out to the garage and promptly handed her what looked to be one of his shirts.

"To protect your clothes from paint splashes," he said.

She had put the shirt on and couldn't help but feel a tingle of pleasure in the knowledge that he had once worn the same shirt.

The next few hours passed by so quickly that they had seemed like minutes to Grace. Dan had already put the undercoat on the cupboard a few days prior, so it was well and truly dry. Dan handed her a paint brush and watching him dip his brush in the emerald green liquid, she followed suit. Before long they had the cupboard painted, although Grace also sported a green tip on the end of her nose from Dan's brush, in response to the two green spots Grace had marked on his dimples.

"Well, that was fun," she said as they began tidying up.

Dan agreed wholeheartedly. "Yep, I think I'm going to have to find some more cupboards to repaint. I must keep the entertainment up for my lady."

Grace felt her heart glow with his words; his lady. He was so romantic. How could she be so lucky? she thinks, as she looks at him, and almost has to pinch herself to believe it was all true.

Although the rain had subsided greatly there was still a constant light drizzle, so, upon Dan's suggestion, they drove to the video shop and hired several movies to watch that night. They then stopped at the supermarket and chose ingredients for their evening meal.

By the time they had cooked and eaten their home-made spaghetti bolognese, and cleaned up, they were more than ready to snuggle up on the lounge to watch the videos they had chosen. And being the gentleman he was, he later drove her home and insisted upon walking her to her front door.

On Sunday, just before lunch time, Dan turned up at Grace's flat to ask her if she'd like to join him in a counter lunch at the Railway Hotel. He notices Rachel lying on the lounge with a book, looking sad. He looks at Grace and gestures with his eyes, looking at Rachel. Grace nods with a smile.

"Rachel, would you like to come with us?" he asks.

Rachel looks up from her book. "Oh no, thank you. I'm fine," she says, attempting a smile.

"Oh come on Rachel, *please*," Grace attempts to coerce her.

"I know Johno is going to be there. Maybe we could play pool?" Dan suggests.

Rachel looks from one face to another, deciding. Grace knows she just doesn't want to intrude on their time together, but now that Dan has mentioned that Johno will be there, she's considering.

"Rachel please come," Grace asks one last time, and Rachel finally makes up her mind.

"Ok, sounds good," she says, and jumps up from the lounge.

They all enjoyed the afternoon, eating, drinking and playing pool. Grace and Rachel beat Dan and Johno, two games out of three, although Grace was convinced the men intentionally lost. But, she wasn't going to mention it, after seeing how happy Rachel was when they won. She had sneaked a side-ways look at Dan and noticed the quick look between the brothers. Yes, she decided, they were more alike than anyone would imagine. Though they hardly looked like brothers, they were very similar in the way they both cared about their friends; and while Johno had the ability to make anyone snap out of a sombre mood with his quick wit and cheeky behaviour, Dan had the ability to make people feel at ease, and seemed to always derive pleasure from doing anything he could think of to make them smile.

She discovered later that Dan had called Johno to confirm he was going to the pub, before coming over to the flat to invite both Grace and Rachel. He had already been thinking about Rachel missing Darel. Grace decides that Dan is the most amazing man she has ever met and can't even imagine her life without him in it now.

# CHAPTER 12

Grace arrived earlier than usual at the tennis courts the following Wednesday night. She was hoping Dan would be early too, so they could spend some time together alone before everyone else turned up. She was aware that his presence in her life was becoming vital to her happiness, although he didn't even need to be there for it to be felt.

Whenever she sits on the lounge in her flat, she instantly remembers Dan snuggling up with her as they watched the movie, Alien, together. When she thinks about Dan in his house, she remembers being wrapped in his arms on his lounge as they watched movies there too. When she imagines being by the river with him, watching the moon, she is once again, held lovingly in his arms. She feels so safe in his arms. It has been a totally new feeling for her, and one she is willing to repeat many times more. But, although she won't be able to snuggle up with him at the Tennis Club, just being close to him will be the next best thing.

She imagines how hard it must have been for Rachel this last week, not being able to be with Darel either at tennis last Wednesday, or on the weekend, because of the flooded Mogiguy Creek bridge. She had been so happy last night, knowing that the water had subsided and he would be coming to tennis tonight. So, when she had passed her racing up the steps to their flat tonight, running late home from work, she had understood why she had had a frown on her face.

"Of all days to run late," she had said breathlessly.

"It's ok Rachel, I'll let Darel know," she had replied, hoping it would make her relax a little.

"Thanks Grace," she heard her yell out from the top of the stairs. "I'll just get changed and I'll be there as quickly as possible."

"OK," Grace had yelled back as she heard the front door to their flat close with a bang. She just hoped Rachel didn't forget to bring her tennis racquet.

She had looked for Dan's Jeep when she drove into the Tennis Courts car park, but she hadn't seen it. Then, after she had parked, she had glanced around for Darel or Johno's utes. But, they weren't there yet either. It didn't matter, she decided. She would just sit at their usual place and wait for them. She wasn't really surprised that Johno hadn't turned up yet anyway because he was usually late. As for Darel, well even though she knew he would be eager to get to town as soon as possible to see Rachel, anything at Binda could have held him up.

As she walks from the car park area to the front of the Club House, she notices a flashy red Citroen drive in. *Nice car*, she thinks, and watches it park as she walks. Then she notices Jasmine alight from it. She groans, but keeps walking, hoping Jasmine hasn't seen her. But, suddenly Jasmine's voice is behind her.

"Oh Grace dear, do wait up. I want to have a chat with you if that's alright. There's something I'd like to ask you" she says so sweetly that Grace hardly recognises her.

Grace turns to face her as she catches up. "Yes, Jasmine," she says, without emotion.

"Well, not right here dear. Why don't we go and make ourselves more comfortable, where you usually sit." she replies, making it obvious it was less of a question and more of an instruction.

Grace is wondering what she wants to ask her, as they walk around to her usual spot at the wooden seating near the courts. The last time she had seen Jasmine was at the Club on the Show night, when she and Dan were leaving. She had wondered how coincidental it had been that she had been sitting with two other women, just after the ladies room incident, and then, the fact that they had all been looking at her as she left. She didn't believe it had been a coincident, although she had no proof the two women with Jasmine had been the same two in the ladies room. She hadn't seen their faces. Besides, even if she did have proof, it wouldn't have been of any benefit. There wouldn't have been any purpose in confronting them. They had only spoken the truth about her being part aborigine, and she had no way of knowing if it were true what they had said about that man named Mark. As for there being any truth about Dan and Jasmine going out together, well it didn't really matter of course. If it were in the past, then it should be left in the past. Besides, Dan had told her that Jasmine was not his girlfriend, and he had proved it over the last few weeks. But, it *would* be interesting to know if they had gone out together in the past. She didn't want to ask Dan, even mention Jasmine's name to him, but – perhaps she could find out for herself. Maybe she could turn this unpleasant situation with Jasmine sitting beside her, to her advantage.

Jasmine couldn't believe her luck. She could not have asked for a better opportunity. She had been determined she would find a way to pass on some information quietly to Grace tonight, and remind her of a few home truths, but she had known her chances were slim. As her tennis partner, Johno was with her most of the time, and when he wasn't, she was with Dan. It had been very annoying, being ousted from Dan's presence between matches. She had had to curb her tongue when he had made it obvious that he wished to be alone with Grace. The hide of him, she thought. Didn't he realise she was only looking out for his best interests? After all, his work was so important to him. Didn't he realise how beneficial it would be for him to marry the daughter of one of the most affluent men in the community, and one who was willing to make him part and parcel of his growing empire? And where was his loyalty anyway, to the man who had helped him get a foot in the door of Council? Her father had had foresight about him. He could always spot the winners. Yet, here Dan was, wasting his time on a half breed aborigine, even if she didn't look anything like one. But, pedigree mattered; surely Dan could understand that, *would* understand that, when he woke up to his senses.

She had thought that if Grace had any quality about her too, she would have taken good notice of that little conversation Cat and Leanne had held in her honour in the ladies room at the Club. It was still too early to tell if it had had any lasting effect on her though, because she hadn't seen either her or Dan since then. However, she has always been one to make the most of an opportunity when it stared her in the face, and she wasn't about to allow circumstances to dictate.

*Every little bit counts*, her mother would often say, even though that was more in context to preening herself in front of a mirror or using her charms to entice people to do what she wanted. Yes, she would just give Grace a few more things to think about in case she still hadn't got the message that it would be best for her to make her permanent departure out of Dan's life, as soon as possible. Better safe than sorry, she thinks. Some people just need more of a push than others. It seems Grace was either quite stupid or she just had more tenacity than she would like to give her credit for. But, no-one gets the better of Jasmine, she concludes.

Grace looks sideways at Jasmine, waiting for her to speak.

"So Grace, tell me, how has your week been?"

Grace sighs. She really doesn't want to indulge in idle chit-chat with Jasmine. All her senses tell her it would be best to be as far away as possible from her at this moment. Sitting here beside her almost feels like tempting fate, she thinks. But, although she knows she could easily just stand up and walk away, ending this conversation before it even really starts, she thinks of Dan. Not only does she want to find out more about Jasmine for herself, she understands that it would be best to remain polite for Dan's sake and not fuel any ill feeling.

"Jasmine, is that what you want to ask me?" she says, trying not to sound impatient.

"No, no dear. I'm just showing manners, that's all. That's how ladies behave, isn't it?"

Grace stares at her, finding it hard to believe her nerve after the way she has behaved in the recent past.

"Hmm, of course Jasmine," she responds very politely, refusing to rise to the bait. "Well, my week has been very busy so far, at work. Where do you work Jasmine?" she asks, feigning interest.

"Oh, you really are new to Dubbo by the sounds of it Grace. Otherwise, you would know that I own a little business in town. Have you heard of - Jazz-Me?"

Grace motions with her head – no.

"Well," Jasmine continues while looking at her nails, "It's a beauty parlour I started up a few years ago. It's essentially for women, but also caters for men. As a matter of fact, Dan has been in," she adds, although she has no intention of telling Grace that he had only come in once for a hair-cut while she hadn't even been there, when the business had first started. And even Jasmine hadn't known that he had done it as a favour to her father, after he had suggested that Jasmine's 'people', as he called the hairdressers on his payroll, were the best in town. He had quietly added though, that it would mean a lot to him if Dan would be one of Jasmine's first customers. "Of course," she continues, now filing her fingernails with a silver nail-file she has pulled from her stylish back pack by her side, "Jaz-Me has only the *best* clientele. I'm very selective. I was going to ask if you had considered visiting Jazz-Me, but I imagine you would realise it really wouldn't be a good idea." She stops filing her nails long enough to reach behind her and briefly touch Grace's hair. "It's very dark, isn't it?" she says looking directly at her face. "I guess we're stuck with our genes."

Grace flinches, but manages to remain calm, despite the fire Jasmine has instantly ignited within her with her words. She decides that despite Jasmine's obvious connotation, she is going to find out what she needs to know. She changes the subject. "So, you've known Dan for quite a while then?"

*Hook, line and sinker*, Jasmine thinks, proud of her ability to get the conversation to exactly where she wants it. "Oh yes dear, I've known Dan for almost all my life. The only time we haven't known each other, was before we started school." She giggles, pretending to make a joke. "We've had our ups and downs of course, along the way, but don't all couples, er, I mean, friends? He can be so annoying at times, but I always end up forgiving him for his lapses of judgement." She looks up and smiles, as if remembering something pleasant. "Perhaps it's because he is such a good kisser. Oh, but of course, you know exactly what I mean?"

At that moment Dan walks up with a concerned look on his face. He sees Grace sitting beside Jasmine, looking decidedly pale and with a sick look on her face. Meanwhile Jasmine has just put something back into her bag. She looks up to see Dan glaring at her.

"Oh Dan, I'm glad you've finally arrived. Grace and I have been having a lovely chat while waiting for you," she says, ignoring the look on his face. "Perhaps you'd like to sit here now, while I go and check to see which Court we're playing on first." She gets up and walks away with a smug look on her face.

Grace doesn't know how she managed to play tennis that night. Jasmine's words kept repeating themselves, around and around in her mind. She had hoped to find out if Jasmine and Dan had ever been a couple in the past. Well, she had not only succeeded in finding that out, but also a great deal more.

Her common sense told her to ignore Jasmine's words. All that really mattered was that Dan was in love with her, and he had proved that on many occasions, especially recently. That was the only thing that mattered, wasn't it? Or, was it the only thing that mattered to *her*? What about Dan? There were other things that mattered to him; especially his work and his reputation within the community. He had worked hard to build those up. Perhaps what those women had said in the ladies room was true. She could see it happening now after what Jasmine had said. Could she live with herself if the same thing happened to Dan? Would he end up hating her? She had pushed these thoughts down before when they had risen, but it seemed they were determined to be reckoned with. Her head was telling her that her relationship with Dan would be doomed now, and her heart was beginning to break.

Dan had been watching her very closely all night. She had somehow pulled herself out of the stupor that Jasmine had left her in when he had appeared; enough to be able to function at least. And thankfully Darel and Johno had appeared just behind Dan then too.

Dan had sat down beside her with worry written all over his face, but she had reached up and gently stroked his cheek with her hand and smiled.

"Hi," she had said, as if she had just noticed he was there.

He had taken her hand from his face and held it firmly between both of his.

"Are you alright Grace?" he had asked with concern.

"Yes, I'm ok. I must have eaten tea too fast. I feel a bit sick in the stomach," she had said, trying to reassure him. It hadn't been a lie; she really did feel like she was going to throw up.

He had not looked convinced, although he nodded, accepting her words.

Darel and Johno had started chatting then, and pulled Dan and Grace into the conversation, until Jasmine appeared and took Dan away to their first match for the night.

Rachel appeared shortly after, having made a bee-line to the Club House on her way to them. She smiled at Grace, telling her the Court number she and Johno had been assigned, and whisked Darel away for their first match.

For the remainder of the night Grace felt like she was in a bad dream, but she knew it was a dream that would haunt her for a very long time, and not one where someone would wake her and tell her everything was ok. Everything was *not* ok, and she could see that it was only going to get worse.

She couldn't compete with Jasmine. It was now evident that Jasmine had been investing in Dan for a very long time. And she had made it perfectly clear, she would not let him go. Through Jasmine's presence in his life, Dan would have everything he needed to ensure a bright future, whereas with her, he would struggle. How could she put her happiness above his? If she told him what Jasmine had said to her, she is sure he would tell her that it was all in the past, and to put it all out of her mind. She can even imagine he might become upset with Jasmine and say something he might later regret.

Jasmine held the ace of all aces over his life; his work and standing within the community. How would he cope with gossip about his *abo* girlfriend, or wife? Would he always be able to restrain himself when people insulted her? Would repeated racist comments, which he would be bound to receive because of her, eventually cause him to crack and lose his credibility in the community. *Oh why did it have to come to this?*

# CHAPTER 13

Grace is relieved she's almost at Jannali. She just wants to curl up in the bed in the guest room and go to sleep. Being awake is too difficult. She's not even sure how she got through the last few days. Her mind is so weary from wrestling with reality and what she had once thought and really wanted to be true.

Despite accepting what she had to do on Wednesday night, she had still held on to a thread of hope that somehow, miraculously, there would be a way to be able to stay with Dan. But, no-matter how much she had begged the heavens to show her a way, it hadn't appeared. And eventually, she had returned to acceptance, and almost drowned in a sea of despair.

She thinks back on the last few days as she drives through Barwon village…

When she had finished her last match for the night on Wednesday, she had asked Dan to walk her to her car. He had still had another match to play in a few minutes time. He looked surprised by her request, because they had normally waited for each other to finish and left at the same time, although in their own vehicles. Most people had gone by then, so they usually had time for a cuddle before they parted.

She had wanted so much for tonight to be like the previous nights, for Dan to hold her and kiss her, but this time, to also tell her that everything was going to be alright. But she knew he couldn't do that, even if he knew what she had learned.

He had gently pushed her back against the car with his body, wrapped his arms around her shoulders and looked deeply into her eyes.

"Are you sure you're alright,' he asked.

She had to do it soon, she decided. It would be so much harder the longer she left it. But how do you tell someone you love that it's over, when you don't want it to be? How is it possible to look into a person's soul, like she feels she is every time she looks into his eyes, and say you no longer care, when it is a lie? How can she do this? She realises that she is going to have to muster up as much courage as she can to pull this off and somehow convince him. She would be going to Jannali on Friday and that would just prolong the pain. *Just, do it*, she bullied herself.

"No, I'm not Dan. I'm not really sure about…" She hesitates.

"About what? he interjects, looking nervous.

"About…us," she finally forced out.

"What do you mean Grace? Everything was fine until I found you talking to Jas…" he stops, looks over to the tennis club and back at Grace. "What did Jasmine say to you earlier?"

"It doesn't matter what Jasmine says anymore Dan." Her lips tremble. "Oh please don't make this any harder than it is," she says, her eyes welling up with tears.

"But darling something has happened, why can't you tell me? Why can't you *trust* me?" he pleads, with his voice, with his eyes, and with his hands, holding her shoulders tight.

She can't bear it anymore. She just wants to fall into his arms and weep. But she can't; not now, not ever.

"It's over Dan," she says, and a sob erupts from her mouth as the tears stream down her face, unchecked.

Dan is looking at her, stunned. She takes the opportunity and pushes him backwards so she can get into her car. She starts the motor and drives off in a frenzy, leaving Dan standing there like a statue.

Rachel and Darel had also had a late match, so thankfully by the time they arrived at the flat, Grace was already in bed. They wouldn't have thought anything of it, because Rachel knew she'd had a busy start to the week and would be tired. By the time Rachel had arrived home though, Grace had cried herself to sleep, dreaming that the second pillow she was cuddling, was Dan.

On Thursday morning, she had almost called in sick for work. She couldn't remember ever feeling so washed out. It didn't even compare to the time just after she had met her mother for the first time, after little sleep the week prior. But then she realised why; with her mother, it had been from emotional joy, with Dan it was from emotional pain.

Rachel had looked at her and asked if she were coming down with something. She had also suggested that perhaps she should call in sick and stay in bed. But Grace knew that that was the last thing she needed. So she went to work.

She was relieved when both Thursday and Friday were also hectic days at work; grateful for small mercies.

After work on Thursday, she arrived back at the flat to discover she was there before Rachel. She was worried that Rachel might discover the real cause of her looking unwell, if she were to spend time with her that night. She needed time to herself for a while, to be able to cry openly without anyone knowing. It had been so hard to keep the tears at bay during work.

Then she had an idea. She could leave a note for Rachel saying she had gone out. Rachel would probably think she was with Dan, so she wouldn't think any more of it. She would tell her what happened soon, but not when it was still so raw. She couldn't bear to talk about it yet.

So she packed a picnic tea for herself, left the note for Rachel and took off in her Corolla. She then drove around town until she found a park she had not visited before. She knew it would not be a good idea to go to the park by the river where she and Dan had been. She couldn't cope if he happened to turn up while she was there. But, in her sadness, she was pleased with the park she chose, and even considered that perhaps she would have enjoyed it, if she hadn't felt so broken. It had a pond with ducks, and it was a small measure of comfort, watching them swim around on the still water. She stayed there until dark approached, and arrived home to find Rachel waiting to speak to her. She said Dan had turned up, looking for her.

"Grace, what's going on?" Rachel had asked straight out.

"Didn't Dan tell you?" Grace replied.

"Tell me what Grace? C'mon - spill. It's me you're talking to," Rachel had said gruffly, although Grace knew she was only concerned.

"We've broken up."

"What! That's ridiculous," Rachel retorted, but then had a thought, "Oh, did he break up with you?" she said more gently.

"No, I broke up with him."

"Grace, are you out of your *mind*! You love him; anyone can see that, *and* that he loves you." Rachel paused and sighed. "I'm sorry Grace. I'm just so shocked," she then said, wrapping her arms around her. Grace had then burst into tears and wept on her girlfriend's shoulder.

Rachel had encouraged her to sit on the lounge then and went in search of a box of tissues. She returned with both the tissues and a glass of water. She asked her if Dan had done anything to hurt her, to which Grace had replied with an emphatic – *No!* and become even more upset. Rachel had apologised for asking her that, believing without doubt that Dan would never do anything to hurt anyone, let alone the woman he so obviously loves. Rachel looked so confused, but Grace just couldn't tell her everything.

"What did Dan say?" Grace asked Rachel.

"Well, he just asked if he could speak to you. He didn't look his usual self either, come to think of it. I was surprised of course, thinking you were with him. I just told him that I had arrived home to find you'd left a note saying you had gone out. He just looked very strained, and left."

She then told Rachel that she just couldn't talk about it yet, and Rachel had accepted that, although she told Grace to remember she was there for her to talk to whenever she wanted. They had then both gone to bed, although for Grace it had been another night of tossing and turning.

The next morning, she managed to get out of bed, knowing that at the end of the day she would be going to Jannali. It was something she was now looking forward to. She just wanted to get as far away from Dan as possible at the moment, and she needed a hug from her mother.

She turns the Corolla into the Jannali front drive, and takes a big breath, expelling it as she makes her way through the bushy trail to the Homestead. Her mother is waiting out the front. *She always knows when I'm arriving,* Grace thinks, *even though I don't tell her what time it will be.*

Grace pulls up, gets out of the car and walks over to her. She falls into her arms in a deep hug until Mary disengages and pushes her back far enough to look fully into her face.

"Hello daughter," she says. "It time!"

Mary led Grace through the house and out the back to the seat beneath the old gum tree. It was obvious Grace was upset, but Mary would wait until she was ready to talk about it. And just like the time when they had first met at Biddybungie Reserve, she started to talk about anything other than what might be on her mind, to try to settle her.

Mary pointed excitedly to the sunflowers, their faces smiling towards the sun. She told Grace that she had walked out early this morning as usual, to sit under the tree while the kookaburras laughed, and discovered they had opened up. She said they knew Grace was coming, and they had waited for her, because they knew they were her favourite flowers.

Grace tried to smile, but a tear slipped from her eye, and then she began to talk. She told Mary that she and Dan were no longer seeing each other; that they had broken up on Wednesday. She knew she had to offer some kind of explanation otherwise her mother would probe her until she did. So, avoiding her eyes, she told her that she had just decided that although it had been good in the beginning, she could now see that it wouldn't work out in the long run. She said she was upset because she knew she had hurt Dan, and even if they were not going to be in a relationship, she still cared about him. She felt she had told the truth, even though she had left a lot out.

Mary had watched her closely as she talked, noting the way she refused to look at her. When Grace had finished talking, Mary remained quiet and Grace looked up, puzzled by her silence.

"So, that the story you sticken' to?" she had asked flatly.

Grace didn't know what to say. She chided herself. Had she really expected her mother not to read between the lines? She may not speak well to white man's standards, but her mother was far more astute than most people she knew. And she was the most down to earth person Grace had ever met. Her mother would tell you how it was, no qualms, and you'd better be telling the truth, or watch out. Grace momentarily thinks of Darel and imagines that he wouldn't have had Buckley's chance of being dishonest as a child. She looks at her mother, shrugs her shoulders, and grimaces. She just can't tell her the full story. It would open up a discussion about the issue about being part aborigine, and she doesn't want her to know that being part aborigine has a great deal to do with her unhappiness.

Mary puts her arm around her, and they sit there until the kookaburras start to laugh. But this time, neither Grace nor Mary laugh in return.

Grace walks into the guest bedroom, where she has slept many nights before. She puts her small bag, containing what she needs for the weekend, on the chair in the corner. She then sits on the bed and leans forward, resting her elbows on her knees, her hands covering her face. Mary walks in and sits close beside her, placing her arm around her shoulders.

"It be alright daughter, you see," she says reassuringly.

Grace notices something new on her bedside table. She picks up the hand-made doll and studies it. It is made of dark brown material and dressed in a brightly coloured dress, depicting circular patterns and swirls of brown surrounded by yellow dots, and splotches of aqua, teal and coral. Her hair is black and she has a sweet smile on her face. There are white dots on her cheeks, forehead and around her wrists.

"Did you make her Mum?"

"Yeah, for you. I been waitin' to give her to you. Never too old for a doll, hey?" she chuckles.

Grace looks at her mother tenderly. "Thank you. She's beautiful."

"She a Buuja-Buuja doll; aborigine woman. Buuja-Buuja, mean butterfly. She watch over you when I not around Grace," Mary says patting her leg and standing up. "There be many watchin' over you daughter. You just got to let them know you know they's there," she adds, as she walks out of the room and heads to the kitchen to prepare tea. Don will be home soon.

Grace thinks about her mother's words. She really doesn't know much about her mother's ways and she really hadn't been very receptive when she first arrived at Jannali. She had listened, but she had felt like it was all something from long ago; that it couldn't really apply to her life today. Besides, she looked white, had grown up as a white person, and wasn't it all because of being part aborigine that had caused all her problems in the first place? First she had been taken from her mother, then adopted, and now she had lost the man she loves; all because she was part aborigine. Why would she want to embrace the aborigine way of life? Why should she?

She looks at the butterfly doll in her hand. It now feels heavy, adding to the weight of the sorrow in her heart. Although it was made and given in love, she now feels it to be a token of her pain. She wants to put it in one of the cupboards out of sight, but she doesn't want to offend her mother. She places it back on the bedside table, but turns its face to the wall.

She leans back onto the bed. It feels so inviting. She decides to rest her eyes for a few minutes.

She must have dozed off. She wakes, hearing Don's voice. She gets up and goes to the kitchen.

Don is sitting at the kitchen table and she goes over to him, bends down and pecks him on the cheek. As she straightens, she looks into his eyes and notices they look a little sad.

"Good to see you Grace," he says, but she has a feeling her mother has already told him about Dan. He doesn't seem his usual self.

"What have you been up to?" Grace asks, hoping to get him thinking about something else.

"Oh, mostly trying to get some fencing repairs done. One of the old gums close to the fence at the front paddock fell two days ago. Made a right mess of the fence. Then I noticed a couple of the ewes poking around in the scrub. But, it'll be right, I'll get it sorted."

Grace nods. "In the mood for a game of chess later," she asks.

"Now, as I recall, you won last time, right?"

"Yep," she says, smiling.

"Well, I can't let that go unchallenged," he replies with a big grin.

After they finish tea, Grace insists on washing up. Then Don sets up the chess-board.

Mary listened to them playing while she worked on some mending. She occasionally looked up to catch Grace with a far-away look on her face, or like she was struggling to hold back tears, while Don concentrated on his next move.

When they all decided to call it a night, Grace hugged them both and headed for bed. She was just about to shut the bedroom door when Mary appeared.

"I been wonderin' daughter. How 'bout we go for a walk down to the river tomorrow. Whadda think?"

"Yeah, sure Mum. That sounds nice."

Mary leans forward and pecks her on the cheek. Grace reciprocates. Mary turns to go, but then half-turns back to her.

"You know, sometimes runnin' don't do nothin' but make your legs tired. Think 'bout that as you go to sleep. Good night, daughter."

---

Grace slept fitfully, tossing and turning as her dreams took her to places she knew she had been to before, but she couldn't recognise. At one time she was walking through a bushy area and the trees were people with branches for arms, reaching out to touch her as she manoeuvred to elude them. At another time she was adrift in a large river when suddenly a giant wave of water fell on her and she struggled to avoid being dragged into its murky depths. Eventually, she found herself running through the night, but she didn't know what she was running from. She turned, to look behind her, but she couldn't see anything but an eerie darkness. But there *was* something there; she could feel it. Why couldn't she see it? She focused on the track ahead, propelled forward by the fear of what followed behind, until she came to a fork in the road. She stopped and glanced behind her again. Still nothing, but she knew something was there, lurking in the darkness. She had to get away from it as far and as fast as possible. Decision, decision; which way should she go? She looked first one way, and the other, but no matter how hard she tried to make a choice, she couldn't. She could feel whatever it was behind her getting closer and closer. Hurry, hurry, which way should she go? She had to choose, but then it was too late. It was there! She felt it latch on to her and she screamed - and woke up.

"Grace, it alright daughter. I here, your mother here, hush, hush."

Grace clung to Mary and sobbed and sobbed, until exhaustion took over and she fell back to sleep.

# CHAPTER 14

Grace had to tell Mary everything. She knew it the moment she woke up the next morning. With her dream still vivid in her mind, and how she had wept in her mother's arms afterwards, she realised she needed help. She still wasn't sure what that help entailed, but she couldn't cope with the way things now were, the indecision, the turmoil, the heartbreak.

After breakfast, they went for a walk to the river as planned, and she was just about to start up a conversation, when a kangaroo jumped in front of them with a baby in her pouch. The kangaroo looked at both Mary and Grace and then turned and hopped away.

Grace smiled. "That was so nice, wasn't it? Did you see the baby in her pouch Mum?"

"I sure did, and now I tell you the dreaming story about how the kangaroo got her pouch."

They continue to saunter along the track as Mary begins...

"This story is about a mother kangaroo, her baby Joey and an old wombat:

*'When the world was young, the mother kangaroo didn't have a pouch like she has now. Not having a pouch made it hard for her to look after Joey because as soon as her back was turned her baby would*

*wander off exploring.*

*One day an old and grumpy wombat turned up. He kept complaining, over and over, about being weary and blind, and not having a friend in the world. When he told the mother kangaroo that he hadn't had anything to drink or eat for days, she felt sorry for him, even though he wouldn't stop grumbling. She told him she would be his friend and help him. She told him to hold onto her tail and she would take him to water and food.*

*So off they went, although it took a long time to get to where she wanted to take him, because the old wombat had trouble holding onto her tail. She had been very patient. But, by the time the old wombat was drinking and eating, she realised she needed to get back to Joey.*

*So she took off, and after searching high and low, she finally found him asleep under an old gum tree. She figured he was alright, so she bounded back to where she had left the old wombat to make sure he was still alright too.*

*The mother kangaroo was almost back to where she had left the old wombat when she sensed danger. Then she spotted a hunter moving close to the old wombat, so she made a lot of noise to distract him and led him far away, until the hunter finally gave up and went home.*

*By now, she was worrying again about Joey, so she bounded back to where she had last seen him, and with great relief found him still asleep under the old gum tree. She woke him and together they made their way slowly back to where she had left the old wombat. But no matter how much they searched they couldn't find him.*

*The reason they couldn't find the old wombat is because he had in fact been, Biyaami, the Creator Spirit, who had come down from the sky to test the kindness of his creatures.*

*The mother kangaroo was* rewarded *for her kindness. Biyaami presented her with a dilly-bag to tie around her waist, so she could carry Joey wherever she went. When she tied it to her waist though, the dilly bag magically turned it into a pouch.*

*From then on, Joey could be kept safe and she need not worry about him getting lost again; she could take him with her wherever she went.'*

"Thanks Mum," Grace said when she had finished. "That was nice."

"Ok. Now what you got goin' on with your man, for starters?"

It was a good place to start Grace decides. It was easy to talk about the man you love; the words flowed freely from her lips and her eyes sparkled. She talked about how his smile made her heart do somersaults, his touch made her skin tingle, and his eyes caused her to bare her soul. She said he treated her like a lady, sang love songs to her, and when he held her in his arms she felt safe and cherished. She said he loved his work with a passion and he was dedicated and conscientious in all that he did. She told Mary that she loved him to the moon and back, but she could never be with him.

Mary had stopped walking then and turned to Grace with a questioning look. Grace quickly added, "I'll tell you why, don't worry," she said, and sighed deeply.

So she told her about Jasmine. She told her that Jasmine was from a wealthy family who had a foothold within the community. She said that Jasmine had known Dan all her life, had grown up with him and wanted him as her man. She told her that Jasmine was the daughter of Councillor Healy, a former Council employee in a managerial position who had helped Dan when he first started working there. And Dan felt indebted to him. She said that Jasmine had caused her problems.

"What sorta problems?"

She hesitated, but knew now that she had come this far, there was no turning back.

"Hang on. Let's get over to that log so we can sit down," Mary said, pointing to the other side of the fence.

They had arrived at the river, and the dividing fence of Jannali and Binda. Grace followed Mary as she stepped around the big river gum, where the fence ended near the river bank, and walked across a grassy area to a big log.

"This is where Rachel and Darel be married Grace," Mary said as they sat down.

"It's a lovely spot," Grace said looking around. "Perhaps I shouldn't be talking about bad things here though. You know, would it be like a bad omen or something?

"Now, that my girl, you know more than you think. But, it ok, 'cause what you got goin' on, be fixed. 'Sides, this place seen a lot more than *your* tears daughter, hmm, that for sure." Mary starts to go off into one of her wistful moods, but Grace pulls her back with her next words.

"Mum, you don't even know what I'm going to say yet. How do you know that it can be fixed."

"Grace, you think I born the other day?"

"Yesterday," Grace corrects her.

"What?"

Grace shakes her head. "It doesn't matter."

"Well now, you might as well spit it out cause things need to be straightened out, that for sure."

Grace doesn't believe anything can be 'straightened out', especially after she tells her what she's about to. And the last thing she wants to do is offend her mother. She's starting to regret her decision to tell her everything now.

"I can tell it's not somethin' you want to tell me, but unless you get it out it's gunna rot inside of ya. When I lost you all them years ago I kept that pain inside for a long, long time, and it was eatin' away at me insides somethin' terrible. I was a stolen child too Grace. You think I haven't seen what white people can do to us? Let it out daughter…

"But, it's just that - I feel ashamed," she blurts out.

"Go on," Mary says quietly.

"Well, it's hard to tell you this Mum, because I don't want to upset you. I don't want you to think that I don't love you, admire everything about you," she starts.

"I knows that daughter. You wouldn't be here if you didn't," she replies gently. "It ok, I'm tougher than you thinks, c'mon, get it out."

Grace still doesn't know quite how to tell her, so she takes the indirect approach.

"Jasmine made me realise I'm not good enough for Dan. You see…"

Mary interrupts, "Hang on, another woman say you no good for Dan, and you believes her? *Why?*"

"Because, well… because I'm part aborigine" she says and hangs her head.

"Hmm, they sure did a good job on you, that for sure." Mary replies without hesitation. Grace thinks she means Jasmine, but Mary makes it clear. "You grow up thinking you know who you are, a white girl in a white family, and then out of the blue, you get told they not your people and you got aborigine in you. Then, on top of that, they let you know they think it bad. It no wonder you don't feel proud of the aborigine in you." She pauses to see that Grace wasn't expecting her to understand, but the relief shows instantly; in her shoulders suddenly relaxing and her face looking instantly less strained.

"Now, I grow up an aborigine; my mother, your grandmother, was aborigine, Wiradjuri, 'though my father was white. But my mother, grandmother and me, we know who we was and we proud of it. But, the white people take me and tell me it no good being Wiradjuri. I go along with them, 'cause I got no choice, but alls they did was make me not like white people, for long time. And - I 'shamed to be nearly white." Mary notices Grace listening intently.

"So, here we both with same problem; feeling 'shamed. So waddha we goin' do about it? 'Caus it no good feelin' 'shamed; it do you no good." Mary pauses to give Grace time to think.

"You see daughter, no matter what people tell you or do to you, you gotta remember you can still keep what's inside." Mary takes Grace's hand and places it on her heart. "No-one can take that away, unless you let them; that important part. When you look at it, it a good thing we not fully white or fully black, 'cause we the ones who understand both sides. We got to use that in our lives; be proud of that. We just got to remember, never forget, and that what I tryin' to do for you, just like I did for Darel."

Grace is a bit stunned by Mary's words. She hadn't thought about it like that before. She's still rolling it around in her mind, when Mary continues, "Now, it don't seem to me that Dan was worried about your mother being part aborigine when I met him a few weeks back. I reckon he would have high-tailed by now, if he did. Anyway, don't you realise that he a friend of Darel's? Now Darel, your brother, same as you, but different father, he marryin' Rachel soon, and she all white. Same thing, Don and me, an' we alright. You thought about that?"

"Yeah, I know, but it's just that it's a bit different in Dan's case. He has to work in town and get on with the people in town…"

"Hmm, does he? Or, do they need to get on with him? Maybe they all need to work it out to get on together. 'Sides, seems to me, Dan the type of fella make his own choice, an' you sure he not made it already?"

Grace ponders on Mary's words. "But, you don't know Jasmine Mum. She's…well, she's…"

"No I don't, but Dan does. Seems to me you got a bit a talkin' to do with that man of yours. You can't leave him in the dark about how you feeling, 'specially if he wants to be with you for the rest of his life. I told Don, everything 'fore he proposed ta me. No point in startin' off together hidin' stuff in ya heart. Sooner or later it come out, and bite ya on the bum."

Grace smiles despite Mary's serious words. Mary may not have the most eloquent way of explaining things, but she gets the point across. Grace is quiet, reflecting on their conversation. She looks directly at her mother with a look of repentance on her face.

"Mum, I'm sorry for not bringing this up before. I guess I just didn't want you to be disappointed in me. I did try to take in all that you and Darel tried to teach me when I first came to Jannali."

"You not disappoint me daughter," she replies putting her arm around her and giving her a firm hug. "A lot of what you know already in here," she point to her heart. "And, I not finished with you yet, anyway." She pauses for a moment. "You see Grace, it important to me that you learn about the Wiradjuri way, cause it still part of you, no-matter how much you think it cause problems. It something you can't run away from any more than a kookaburra can run away from its tail-feather. Just remember, it was the white man who came and take our family, our land, our language - our identity, from us. We got nothin' to be shamed of." She turns and looks directly at Grace. "I will talk about Wiradjuri ways because I don't want them to get lost forever. I want my children to know so they can tell my grandbabies. But, it up to you how you live your life. You understan' daughter?"

Grace wraps her arms around Mary, giving her a huge squeeze. "Yeah, I do now. Thank you Mum."

Mary's eyes glaze over. "Good, good." she says as they disengage. "Now, what you gunna do about this man of yours?"

Grace looks sadly out to the water. "I told him we were through.

It's too late."

"It never too late to speak your truth Grace; no matter what happens."

# CHAPTER 15

Saturday night, Grace felt far more relaxed than she had in days. Her heart still ached from parting with Dan the way she had, but at least now she had a better understanding of why she had broken it off with him. She had allowed Jasmine to take advantage of the fact that she had felt ashamed of being part aboriginal. She had allowed Jasmine to influence her to break it off with Dan. However, after her discussion with her mother, she no longer felt ashamed, or guilty for feeling that way; the veil had been lifted from her eyes.

When her mother confessed to her own feelings of shame about being part white, Grace realised that they both must have experienced similar feelings to thousands of aborigines from mixed descent. She now viewed her aborigine heritage in a completely new light.

Her mother had said; *We got nothin' to be 'shamed of,* and Grace could now see she was right. Instead of feeling inferior for being part aborigine, she should be feeling proud; proud that she was a descendent of a race of people who had defied being obliterated by white man.

So, she wondered, should she then feel ashamed for also being a descendant of the same race of people who had tried to destroy her aborigine ancestors? Perhaps that would be more appropriate. After all they had been the instigators.

But feeling ashamed for the actions of her white ancestors would still leave her in the same boat, and wouldn't serve any other purpose than to keep her stuck in an endless cycle of feeling unworthy.

Therefore, she needed to reconcile herself to accept both sides of her ancestry, unconditionally, and by doing that, discover the person she really was.

She was just about to turn the light off in her bedroom to go to sleep when she noticed the Buuja Buuja doll facing the wall on her bedside table. She picked her up and looked into her face, and smiled, then gently placed her back; this time with her eyes to the front.

Late Sunday morning Grace walked along the track, past the big gum tree at the dividing fence, and on to the house at Binda. She knew Rachel would take the same track to Jannali at some time to see her before going back to Dubbo, but she was eager to see Darel too.

Rachel would have arrived at Binda on Saturday morning, as she had told Darel she would, but Grace hadn't wanted to interrupt her time alone with him then. It was a good thing she hadn't made this visit yesterday anyway, because her thoughts had changed considerably since she had spoken to her mother.

Originally, she had planned to speak to Rachel and Darel, to tell them why she had broken it off with Dan. She had felt that it would have been difficult to tell them that it all had to do with her being part aborigine, because her brother was just like her, part aborigine, and Rachel was marrying him. She had thought they might both be offended by it. But, after talking to Mary, her agenda had changed, and she was eager to discuss things with them.

By the time she walked up to the house yard gate, they had been loudly informed of her approach. The dogs barked a welcome and came over to say hello as she swung the house gate open. They remembered her from when she had lived at Binda with Darel, before she had moved to Dubbo with Rachel. She breathed in deeply and was rewarded with the beautiful floral scent of the white rose hedge which clung to the fence.

Rachel opens the front door with a wide grin. "Hi!" she says, and waits for Grace to walk up the footpath and met her at the door.

"I'm not interrupting?" she asks politely.

"Nooo, come in, come in," she says, grabbing Grace's arm and pulling her inside. "Would you like a cuppa, we're just having one," she asks, turning to the cupboard and reaching in for another mug, not even waiting for a reply.

"Ok. Thanks." Grace says, and smiles at Darel.

"Hi Gracie." He pulls his mug away from his mouth and places it in front of him on the table. "What's happenin'?" he asks with curiosity on his face.

"Yes, well, I figure I should let you know what happened with Dan." She pulls out a chair and sits down.

"Well, it's really none of our business," Darel replies. "But, it is a bit of a shock," he adds, looking concerned.

Rachel hands Grace a mug of tea, with the same look on her face as Darel, and sits down next to him.

Grace explains to Darel and Rachel how she had felt ashamed of being part aborigine, but also guilty for feeling that way. She told them that Jasmine had used it to manipulate her into breaking it off with Dan.

"Oh, she can be a nasty piece of work, that one," Rachel had responded, frowning.

"Yes, she's not the sort of person you want to get on the bad side of, that's for sure," Grace replied. "But, it really was my fault for allowing her to take advantage of my weakness."

"Don't be too hard on yourself Gracie," Darel said. "It's not easy sometimes." The two girls look at him questioningly. "Being part aborigine," he adds, and they both nod.

"Well, I had a long talk with Mum yesterday, and she made me see things I hadn't before; she made things a lot clearer for me."

"Good," Rachel said, and Darel nodded.

"You see, I now realise that the fact that I was worried about how Dan would be affected with me in his life, was showing me that I needed to get myself sorted; my thoughts straight," she said looking at them both with tears starting to well up. "So, it wasn't really Jasmine's fault that I broke it off with Dan. It was mine!" She looks down at the mug of hot steaming tea in front of her. "And now I've lost him," she says quietly, as a tear runs down her cheek.

Rachel is by her side in a flash, hugging her from behind. "Oh Grace, I'm so sorry you're hurting," she says as her own eyes now glisten with tears.

"Gracie, it's not too late, you know," Darel says with confidence. "Dan's not the type of bloke who gives up easy and especially once he sets his mind to something," he adds. "I've known him a long time, and I can tell ya, he doesn't say something unless he means it and he can't be swayed once he's made up his mind. *And*, he's always been right choosy about women. I could easily have seen him on his own for the rest of his life, if you hadn't come along."

Although Grace is instantly encouraged by what Darel has just said, it also makes her feel like a heel. To think, he trusted her with his heart, not something he easily shares, and she stomped on it.

It did make a lot of sense though, about Dan being stubborn. She had seen first-hand the way he stood up for her and Darel, and she had only just told her mother yesterday how dedicated and conscientious he was in all that he did.

Grace decides she needs to take her mind away from the hurt she was feeling for Dan, and talk to Darel about the other matters she had on her mind. "Did anyone ever give you a hard time about being part aborigine Darel, like when you were growing up?"

Rachel gives Grace another quick squeeze and returns to her seat.

Darel looks towards Rachel, and Rachel nods.

"Well, Rach's mother didn't like me from the beginning. She tried to separate us. That was one reason she sent Rach to boarding school. In the earlier days, when we were both still in primary school at Barwon, she didn't hold back about how she felt, and a lot of kids at school were told by their parents not to have anything to do with me. Rach and I didn't know about it then of course, and we didn't care anyway, about those other kids. Did we darlin'?" He looks over at Rachel and smiles tenderly. "Rach has always been my best friend," he adds proudly. Rachel reaches over and caresses his hand. "Anyway," he says turning to Grace again, "I looked white, just like Dad, but Rach's mother couldn't get over the fact that Mum was part aborigine." He pauses, thinking. "You see Gracie, things were a lot tougher for anyone who looked aborigine in any way, back then. People in the community were a lot more racist back in those days. Rach's mother had been a friend of Dad's first wife, Vivienne, who everyone called Viv. Viv and Dad were well respected in the community; after all, they were the Rutherfords of Jannali. So, when Viv died from cancer, everyone in the community was shocked that Dad married his housekeeper, who also happened to be part aborigine. None of them knew how close Viv and Mum had become. They were the best of friends. Mum told me all this only recently. She came to have a talk with me because she had just visited Viv's grave at the Barwon cemetery. She said she had to go tell Viv about you, Gracie. She said she could just see Viv's face, smiling with happiness for her. Apparently Viv and Dad were the only ones who had known about you for a long time. She hadn't felt safe to look for you until fairly recently."

Grace interrupts, looking a bit confused. "What do you mean that she felt safe to look for me? She's been married to Don for a long time now."

"Yeah, Dad would never let anything happen to Mum, you know that, but it took a long time for her to get rid of feeling scared of white people in authority. She told you about how she was taken to a Home? he asks.

"Yes, she told me about that. It must have been so awful." Grace says sadly.

"Ok. Well, even white people, not in authority, were still really against aborigines of any colour back then you see. A lot more than they are today. That's another reason why Mum doesn't like going into town much. At first she didn't mind. It made her feel independent driving by herself into Dubbo and back. She would also drive in to watch me in sport events, and even drive me to other towns to compete. She used to see the other aborigine mothers from Dubbo a lot by doing that too. Anyway, she tried to be friendly to them, wanted to find out if they were from her family's tribe, or even had any idea where you might be, but they snubbed her. And then this one aborigine bloke I played cricket with did the same to me when I tried to find out a bit about his family. He was suspicious of me because I looked white, and the same thing happened to Mum on a different level. They were suspicious of her because she was only half aborigine. You see Gracie, we're in the middle and both sides feel a bit uncomfortable around us; maybe not even realising it. It takes time to build friendships in the bush as it is, so with our added 'difference' it's usually harder. It seems to me though, that Dan's not worried about it one-iota." He looks at Grace and watches her thinking about what he has just said, and picks up his mug to take a mouthful of tea. "Does that answer your question?" he asks, and swallows a mouthful.

"Yeah, thanks," she answers, looking down into the hot liquid in her mug. Darel drains his tea and stands up, bending down to give Rachel a cuddle and a peck on the cheek. "I'd better get back to it," he says. "I'll be back before sunset," he adds, and he walks around and rubs Grace affectionately on the shoulder. He knows she's still thinking about all he's just said. He walks out of the kitchen.

Rachel looks across at Grace on the other side of the table. She places her hand on top of Grace's. "Are you ok?" she asks gently.

Grace looks up, into her eyes. "Yeah, thanks." Rachel removes her hand from Grace's. "It's just that I realise now how tough you all had it; you and Darel, as well as Mum. I feel like I really don't have an excuse for feeling sorry for myself. Because, that's what I've been doing," she says looking anguished.

"Grace, you've got every reason to have felt the way you did, but I reckon you need to stop blaming yourself the way you are"

Grace nods in affirmation. "Yep, you're right. There's no point in continuing to do that," she says and sighs. She decides to change the subject. "Do you think…well, you know what Darel said about Dan being cautious in love?"

"Hmm?" Rachel is wondering where Grace's question is leading to.

"Well, do you think I might have frightened him away? I mean, I know I really hurt him," she says, remembering the look on his face when she had broken it off with him at the tennis courts. Tears start to roll down her cheeks.

Rachel gets up from her chair and once again goes around to Grace. She slides a chair closer to her and sits down, wrapping her arms around her. Grace leans forward and buries her face in Rachel's shoulder, and sobs.

Rachel murmurs, "It's ok, everything will be alright."

After a few minutes, Grace sits back up. Rachel gets up and walks around to the kitchen counter and comes back with a box of tissues.

"It's a good thing you always have tissues on hand," Grace says, trying to brighten up as she mops up her tears.

Rachel smiles. "So, you're coming back to town on Tuesday then?" she asks.

"Yeah, I promised Mum I'd stay till then. By the way, I'm sorry I didn't do my share of the cleaning before I left."

"Don't be silly, there wasn't much to do. Besides, you've done it for me when I've taken off early to come to Binda." Grace looks a bit ragged from all her crying and Rachel makes a decision. "Let's go back to Jannali. I was coming to see you after a cuppa, but you showed up here first. I can spend the arvo with you and then have tea with Darel before I go back to town."

"Ok," Grace says, draining the remainder of her tea. She then gets up and takes her mug to the sink. "Hey, how many days left before your wedding now? I bet it's really starting to get to you, being away from Darel and having to do all this driving back and forth."

"I decided last week that I'm not going to keep watching the calendar. Try not to think about it. I figure the time might go faster that way."

"Liar!" Grace responds affectionately.

"Yeah well, you know me too well," she answers back, rolling her eyes. "Four hundred and fifty six," she confesses.

"Why are you and Darel putting yourselves through the long wait?

It's obvious you two are meant to be together."

Rachel looks down, and Grace wonders if she should have asked. It really wasn't any of her business. She was just about to tell Rachel that, when she looked up and responded.

"I know it may seem strange. Well, it's for a couple of reasons. I don't want to leave Dad and Mum in the lurch. I mean, they'll need to find someone to take over from me at the store, plus I'll probably have to train the new person. Mum used to fill in when I was at TAFE part-time, but now I'm there full-time, she doesn't come near the place. And then she's still upset by the wedding. She'll probably never get used to Darel and me being together. But, although she'll just *have* to, I guess I'm just hoping she might come 'round, even just a bit, before the wedding. You know, I'd like to see her at least smile on my wedding day. And then, even though Darel's father doesn't care about it, Darel wants to wait until he's twenty-one, out of respect. It was his father's original intention to give him Binda once he was twenty-one. He'll be twenty-one the month before the wedding. And, then there's *you*, Grace. Darel and I both want to see that you're ok before I leave town. And I guess you're going to have to get another flatmate or move. See what I mean?"

"Oh Rachel, you really are the most considerate person in the world, putting your wedding date off because of everyone else. But, don't worry about me. I'll sort something out."

"Well, I would love to get married on Valentine's Day and it doesn't fall on a Saturday until then, so that's another reason to wait," Rachel replies.

\*\*\*

"This is where you'll become Mrs Rutherford," Grace says, smiling at Rachel as they arrive at the grassy area, short of the dividing fence between Binda and Jannali.

Rachel grins sheepishly. "Yeah!" She walks over to the big log that Grace and Mary had sat on the previous day. They both sit down and look out into the water of the river in front of them, both instantly lost in their own thoughts.

A few minutes pass, and then Grace says softly. "Mum said Darel taught you about the Wiradjuri culture."

"Hmm, yep," Rachel replies. "He started telling me about it when we were really little. He told me lots of words for things, like snake - *gadi*, kangaroo - *wambuwany*, kookaburra – *gugubarra*; and all these stories called 'dreamings' he said your Mum told him. But I wasn't to tell anyone. I later realised why they had to be kept secret," she adds, her voice trailing off.

"Mum's told me a little. Well actually, she's told me a lot more than I remember. I guess I didn't really pay much attention when I first arrived at Jannali."

"Well, you had a lot to contend with you know; finding your mother, then meeting Don and Darel." She grins, "Then me, and Johno…" She chuckles. "Then Dan," she adds softly.

"Yeah, I guess."

"You know, I'll never forget the time I was at Jannali homestead and I saw a new painting of a rainbow on the wall. It was so beautiful, so colourful. Have you seen it anywhere?" she asks Grace.

"Yeah, I know the one you mean. It's in the guest bedroom on the wall opposite the bed now. It's the first thing I see every morning when I wake up after sleeping there. "

"Nice!" Rachel replies and looks briefly at Grace, before returning her gaze to the water. "I love that painting, and when I first saw it I was intrigued; the way the colours exploded in the middle with all these different birds flying out from it." She pauses. "I told Darel about it later and he told me that it was a dreaming painting. He told me the story. He said it was based on the dreaming of how the birds got their colour. Do you want to hear it?

"Ok," Grace says, nodding.

"Well, it goes something like this... *'At first the rainbow arch was only fairly small, but it began to suck in more and more red, blue, green, yellow and purple colours from all around, and grow and pulsate. Eventually, it grew so big, it exploded. The rainbow became a million pieces that floated in the air as they slowly drifted toward the ground. And as the million colourful pieces fell towards the ground, the pieces then changed into all the birds we know today.*

*Some of the birds, like the crow, didn't like the feeling of falling, and they screamed out in horror, making the sound: Aaahhh, Aaahhh. Other birds, like the kookaburra, thought it was the funniest feeling they had ever had and started to laugh, making the sound: Haahaa, Haahaaa. And still other birds thought it was the most wonderful feeling of all, so they spread their wings wide, opened their throats, and started to sing the most beautiful songs you could ever hear. And that's how the birds got their colours and their voices; because of that rain-bow, way back in the Dreamtime.'*

"That's a great story," Grace responds when Rachel finishes the story and looks towards her.

Rachel looks back to the river. "Yeah, I think it's really cool. I love the dreaming stories," she says softly. "You know, I also think that one is special to my memory because it's the first time your mother gave me a cuddle. I'll never forget that. She saw me looking at that painting and came over and put her arm around me. We stood there together, not saying a word, just looking at the painting. At the time, I think I just thought she was pleased I had liked her painting, but years later, I realised that it must have made her feel so proud that a white girl showed appreciation for a painting inspired by a Wiradjuri dreaming."

Grace suddenly turns her head to look at Rachel, and Rachel looks back at her. "Yeah, you're right there, I reckon." They are both silent for a minute and then Grace asks, "Mum said yesterday that there's been a lot of tears cried in this river. Do you know anything about that?"

"Probably best to ask your Mum, but I do know that I've cried a lot of tears at this river."

Grace looks at her, her face dropping.

"When I found out Mum and Dad were selling Binda, and then I found out Darel knew before me but didn't let on." She suddenly smiles. "But, there is great happiness here too," she says looking at her. "This has always been Darel's and my favourite place; where we shared all our secrets and…well," she pauses, her smile growing wider, "this is where Darel first kissed me," she concludes.

"Ohhh, that's doubly romantic now, and there couldn't be a more perfect reason for choosing Valentine's Day."

"Yeah, it is," Rachel says, but has another thought. "You know, this is a really special place for many reasons, but I think overall, it's because it has known both immense sadness and incredible joy. And it's because of the sadness that the joy is so much more meaningful. It's like all that energy, good and bad, gets all wrapped up together, each fighting for dominance, but, in the end, it's the joy that wins."

Grace understands more and more, why her brother fell in love with Rachel.

# CHAPTER 16

By Tuesday morning, Grace was eager to get back to Dubbo. She had spent three therapeutic days and three restful nights at Jannali. She couldn't count the first night at Jannali as being restful though, because of her nightmare. However, by Tuesday morning her mind was so much clearer than it had been when she had first arrived at Jannali, she realised that the first night had also been beneficial. It had been the turning point for much needed change.

She looks briefly at the envelope beside her shoulder bag on the passenger seat. She had received it late yesterday. She shakes her head as she thinks back on the previous evening...

Towards sunset, Mary remembers she hasn't checked to see if they had received any mail. As Mary was busy organising tea, Grace offered to walk down to the mail box to check for her. Besides, it was a lovely time of day for a walk. So she headed off down the front drive to the mailbox, enjoying the tree lined front drive and listening to the birds above as they settled for the night. She knew then that she wouldn't even care if the mailbox were empty; she was enjoying the stroll so much.

She was surprised by the number of envelopes in the mailbox as she lifted the lid, but she was even more surprised when she discovered her name written on the top one.

She stood there staring at the front of the envelope as if she could somehow deduce who it was from, even before she turned it over and opened it. She couldn't for the life of her figure out who would write to her at Jannali. All her utility bills were sent to the flat she shared with Rachel in Dubbo. Then it came to her; of course, Susan and Dennis. They were the only ones she had given the Jannali address to before she had left Bathurst.

There must be something wrong, she had instantly thought. She couldn't imagine them writing to her unless that were the case. Should she have cared though? For a few seconds she considered ripping up the letter and throwing it away. But, she scolded herself; that was not a very nice way to be. Susan and Dennis had cared well for her, despite their discrimination tendencies.

So, she turned the letter over and opened it as she walked slowly back up the track. The letter wasn't from Susan and Dennis. It was a neatly typed letter, embossed with letterhead. She stopped to read it…

***

*Simon & Parker Solicitors*
*14A Keppel Street*
*Bathurst NSW 2795*
*Phone: (02) 6360 2203*

*28 November 1979*

*Ms. G. Taylor*
*"Jannali"*

*Barwon NSW 2831*

*To Ms. Taylor,*

*I am writing to you regarding a probate matter. Unfortunately, due to our strict client confidentiality policy, I am unable to disclose the details of the matter in writing. Therefore, I humbly request you make contact with this office via the phone number supplied (above) at your nearest convenience.*

*Yours sincerely,*

*David Simon, Esq.*

*** 

She raced up to the homestead then, almost bumping into Don as he appeared from seemingly, no-where.

"Oh, sorry Don," she said, as she held on to him to steady herself.

"No worries Grace," he replied, a small smile tickling his lips at the humour of it; bumping into each other on a property of over seven thousand acres. But when he noticed the look on her face, his smile faded. "Is everything alright?"

"Oh, I don't know. I just received this letter," she started to say, holding it out to him to take.

"Ok, I'll look at it Grace, no worries, but I need to get me glasses first. They're inside. Let's go," he said, taking her by the elbow and guiding her inside.

"Ok, now let me have a look then," he said once they were at the kitchen table, and he has his glasses on.

"What's going on?" Mary asks, appearing from the hallway at the back of the house. She had been gathering herbs to put into the stew on the stove.

"I received a letter, and I don't know what it's about Mum. Oh, your mail is on the counter there," she says pointing to it.

"Thanks daughter. Now, what's it all about Don?" Mary asks.

"Well, it doesn't give away much; only that it's from someone called David Simon, a solicitor from Bathurst, who wants Grace to contact him." Don looks a little worried. "Grace, have you been in touch with your, um, Susan and Dennis, lately?"

"No. I haven't spoken to them since I left Bathurst. Why?"

"Well, I don't want to alarm you, but this Simon fella wants you to contact him about a Will, from the sounds of it." He watches her face carefully. "Have you had anything to do with any family of theirs?"

Grace's face turns a shade whiter. "No. I, um, I guess I should try to ring the solicitor." Grace suddenly thinks of Rebecca. She may not feel much love for Susan and Dennis any more, but she would feel terrible if anything should happen to them, and especially if Rebecca was left all alone. "There's a number there, isn't there?" she asks Don.

Don looks at the letter quickly, and says, "Yes," as he hands it back to her.

Don looks up at the clock on the wall. "It's almost six forty. I doubt he will still be there, but you never know. Give it a try, anyway."

Mary sits down and starts talking to Don about the letter, while Grace rushes into the hall to ring the phone number.

After several attempts, with no answer, Mary appears beside her.

"It probably be best to try your old home in Bathurst daughter."

Grace nods and starts to ring the number she doesn't need to be reminded of.

Susan picks up. "Hello, Susan Taylor speaking."

"Hello Su..Susan." Grace looks at Mary to reassure her that she has no intention of calling her adoptive mother, Mum, even again. Mary starts to turn to leave, but Grace reaches out and stops her. "How are you?" Grace starts. She didn't even stop to think what she was going to say to Susan if she picked up. At least so far she knows that Susan is alright. She breathes a little slower knowing that Rebecca still has a mother. "How's Den...your husband," she asks.

"Dennis and I are fine thank you Grace. You don't have to worry about not calling us Mum and Dad any more. We know you've found your mother. Besides, you're a grown woman now. Now, is there a specific reason for this call, or are you just ringing to find out how we are?

"No, Yes. I was just wondering how Rebecca is? She might as well find out how her adopted sister is now, as well.

"Rebecca is fine Grace. She's doing very well at school and, as usual, she is a source of joy to Dennis and I." Grace recognises the dig Susan has made at her, but it doesn't faze her now.

"Well, that's good to hear. Is everyone else in the family doing well too?" She decides she'll find out as much as she can.

"Well Grace, I've never known you to feel concern for Aunt Maureen or my mother before. But, yes, they are all doing fine. Now, if you'll excuse me, I'm in the middle of preparing tea. I really must go. Oh, just a minute. I had a phone call from a Mr Symon, Simon, something like that, about a week ago. He was trying to locate you. He said he was a solicitor. I don't know what type of trouble you have got yourself into, but that's no longer my concern. I gave him the address you left here." She seems to be waiting for Grace to respond, but when she doesn't, she says a little more kindly, "Take care Grace," and hangs up.

Grace thinks about her conversation with Susan as she hangs up. At least now she knows it had nothing to do with any of them.

Grace and Mary return to the kitchen table where Don waits patiently. He looks at them expectantly.

"Nuthin," Mary says flatly to Don. "This a real strange thing you got goin' on Grace. Got me stumped," she says.

"Could he have got me mixed up with someone else, do you think?" she looks hopefully at Mary and Don.

"I doubt it Grace," Don says. "The letter is too explicit. You know what sweetheart," he says, waiting for her to look at him. "I don't think it's anything to worry about, now that you know everyone you know is alright."

Grace nods. "Yeah, you're right. I'll call him from the Medical Centre tomorrow on my lunch hour and find out what it's all about."

"Grace, can you…" Mary starts to say, but Grace interrupts.

"Yes Mum, I'll let you know as soon as I know anything. I know you'll be wondering too." She smiles affectionately at her mother.

"Ok then," Mary says, walking around to the stove. "Time to get this stew sorted. You must both be hungry."

Grace turns into the car park of the Medical Centre and glances at her watch. Twenty past eight; she's ten minutes early. She looks across at the letter on the passenger seat. She remembers the last letter she had received that wasn't a bill. It was the letter from her mother, which she had received almost two years ago now. Time has passed so quickly. So much has happened since she met her mother for the first time. Yet, it wasn't all about the events that had occurred in her life either. It was that *she* had changed, although caused by the events. It all had to do with her changed attitude, about being part aboriginal. But, that wasn't all. It was like her changed attitude about her identity had been the key to opening the door where she had hidden so many negative things; fear, self-doubt, self-criticism to name a few. In one way, Jasmine had helped her to open that door. But, had it cost her Dan?

Tomorrow night would be the last tennis night for the comp. She wonders how he will be when she sees him. She wants so much to tell him she's sorry for hurting him the way she knows she did. Will he forgive her? Will they be able to go back to how they were? These questions have haunted her since realisation dawned on her a few days ago. Yes, she had thought Dan would have a better future without her, when she broke it off with him last Wednesday, but she hadn't allowed him to make that decision for himself. She had taken it upon herself to make that decision based on her attitude of not deserving him. She had not known that fully at the time, but she did now. If she had not felt undeserving, she wouldn't have let Jasmine coerce her. She would have fought for him. Was it too late for her to do that now? She knows she will find out when she sees him next, and that could be sooner than

Wednesday night, *if* he had decided he still wanted her in his life. She wonders if he will call around at the flat tonight?

She looks back at the letter again, picks it up and puts it in her shoulder bag. She holds onto her shoulder bag while she alights from the Corolla and heads into work. She hopes they are busy this morning, because she wants the time to pass quickly so she can ring Mr Simon about the letter, at lunchtime. She decides to put it from her mind. It certainly couldn't be as life changing as her last letter, at any rate.

*** 

"Ah hello, Ms Taylor. This is David Simon," the voice down the line says, seconds after the receptionist said she would put her through.

"Hello Mr Simon. How are you?" Grace says, unsure what to say.

He seems slightly amused. "I'm well thank you Ms Taylor."

"Oh good. Um, you asked me to call you, I really have no id…" she begins, but he cuts her off.

"Yes, yes, I'm sure you don't. But may I assure you, there is nothing to be concerned about. In fact I'm sure you will be greatly pleased," he says, and the line goes quiet.

"Ok, well, could you please elaborate?" *I want to know what it's all about, for crying out loud,* she feels like yelling into the phone.

"Well actually, I will need to see you in person for that I'm afraid. I must ask if you would be so kind as to make an appointment with my receptionist."

"Mr Simon, can't you at least tell me *something* now?" she says, now exasperated.

The line is quiet and she is wondering if he has hung up.

"No, I'm very sorry Ms Taylor, but I have been left explicit instructions not to tell you anything, except in person. I can understand what you must be feeling right now..." *no you can't,* Grace almost says out loud... "...but please, again I stress, there is no need for you to be concerned. Ahhh, just one moment please," he says, and once more she's left wondering if they've been disconnected.

He returns reasonably quickly, although to Grace it has felt like minutes. "Now, my receptionist tells me I have some time between 5pm and 6pm this Friday. Would that be suitable?"

Grace realises she's not going to find out anything over the phone, and it's driving her crazy wondering what it's all about. Don did say it must have something to do with a Will, but – *whose?* She thinks that perhaps if she goes along with him, he might give her some indication. She could leave at lunch-time on Friday. She still has several days of leave she hasn't taken this year, so she knows she'll be able to take Friday afternoon off. "Yes, I think that will be ok," she says agreeably.

"Good, good," he says, and he sounds like he is winding down, getting ready to end their call, so she tries one last time. "Mr Simon, is it about a Will?" she asks confidently.

"Well, Ms. Taylor, probate does suggest that," he says carefully. "But, once again, I apologise, but I am not able to elaborate further." He changes from a serious to a chirpy tone of voice. "So then, I'll look forward to meeting you on Friday, Ms Taylor?"

"Yes, I'll see you then. Thank you Mr Simon," she says, and ends the call.

She calls her mother straight away, as promised. Mary is obviously disgusted that Mr Simon hasn't told her anything, but she said Don had warned her. Well, Don had been right, she said, and then got straight onto the topic of going to Bathurst to meet Mr Simon. She didn't ask Grace if she could go with her to the appointment on Friday. She clearly *told* her she was coming with her, and that was that. She said she already had it worked out. She would drive into town and they could go together from there. Grace didn't mind at all. She was glad her mother was coming with her. She would be good company on the two and a half hour journey to Bathurst, and back. So, she'd just have to wait until Friday to find out what it was all about.

The afternoon dragged. She thought perhaps it had a lot to do with thinking about the meeting with Mr Simon on Friday, but when the image of Dan kept coming into her head, she knew it was because she was eager to get back to the flat, in case he turned up. She knew where he lived, but she had no intention of calling around, unexpected, and she didn't want to ring him at work. She wants to see him in person. If he doesn't show up at the flat tonight, at least she knows she will see him tomorrow night at tennis. He and Jasmine had won nearly all their matches, so she didn't doubt they would be in the finals which would be played, being the last night of the comp.

When she finally arrived back at the flat, Rachel was already there. She told her about the letter.

"Wow, I don't know what to say Grace. That's really, really...odd."

"I know, there's really nothing anyone can say, until I find out on Friday. Of course Mum is curious too. I don't blame her, but it's good in a way that I don't know yet, because she wants to come with me to find out."

"I'm glad she's going with you. I would have offered, but we're really busy at the Store."

"That would have been nice too. Thanks anyway though Rachel."

Later that night, when she was in bed trying to sleep, she can't help but feel a little disappointed that Dan didn't turn up. But, then she realises she hasn't been thinking straight. Of course Dan wouldn't turn up. She had broken it off with him. Why would he come around? She then imagines him lying in bed thinking about her. *Oh Dan, I'm so sorry; please don't give up on me*, she imagines him hearing her say, as they both drift off to sleep.

# CHAPTER 17

It was a perfect night for tennis. Grace parked the Corolla in the Club House, car park. She was just alighting from her car when Rachel's car pulled in beside her. She looked around the car park and saw Dan's Jeep, and Darel's and Johno's utes. She also saw Jasmine red Citroen.

She looked over when she heard a car door slam beside her and noticed Rachel watching her. "C'mon, lets go," she said brightly, although she was chewing her bottom lip; a dead give-away that she was feeling nervous.

They walk around to the front of the Club House. Grace can feel her heart beating rapidly. Darel and Johno are sitting in their usual place and they head over to them.

Rachel instantly sits beside Darel and leans in for a kiss. Johno looks at Grace as she sits down beside him.

"Hey Grace," he says smiling.

"Hi!" she says back, and despite feeling nervous, she instantly relaxes. Well, no matter what, she knows Johno will always be her friend, and she's glad of that.

"We only have one match left," he says. "But, we're not in the finals. No surprise there."

"Yeah, but it's been…fun," she replied, though wondered straight away, at her chosen word. Well, it had been fun overall, although most of it had been spent wondering about Dan. But, she'll always remember this competition because it was where she had met Dan; that first night nearly two months ago. She'll always think of tennis in a good light.

"Who's in the finals? Do you know?"

Johno has just taken a swig of his water and was still swallowing, when Darel replies. "Well, so far it looks like, Rach and me, Grace," he says brightly.

"Oh wow, fantastic," Grace replies, smiling. She's now looking forward to watching their match.

"Who else?" she asks, taking a sip of water.

"Dan and Jasmine," Johno replies, and Grace splutters, spitting water everywhere. She had previously thought they would be in the finals, but the mention of their names had caught her off guard.

"Oh sorry," she says to Johno as she coughs. "Must have gone down the wrong way."

Johno just smiles, and heads into the Club House.

Grace looks around as discretely as possible. She hasn't spotted either Dan or Jasmine yet. Johno returns and they all go to various courts. It will be the last match of the tournament for Grace. They lose their match, but leave the courts in a happy mood. They had played well, despite being beaten.

Grace sits down to watch Darel and Rachel battling it out with their opponents. It's a close match by the looks of it. She scans the other courts for Dan. And then she spots him with Jasmine playing on the furthest court away from where she sits. They must have arrived shortly after she had gone out to play. She hadn't seen him although she had occasionally looked over to the Club House during her last match. It looks like they had just finished because she notices the four players shaking hands. She watches as Dan and Jasmine come closer and closer towards her. Her heart starts hammering as she notices him looking at her. He has an intent look on his face: it makes her wince. Several greetings come into her head in readiness. *"Hi Dan, how are you?"* No, that sounds as if she is trying to pretend nothing happened last Wednesday night. *"Hello Dan, good match just then."* No, that sounds a little patronising. *"Hello."* Yes, that will do. That is, if he even acknowledges her.

Then, he's there standing in front of her. She looks up to his face. "Hi!" she says, not being able to find anymore words, after all.

"May I sit down?" he asks, indicating a space on the wooden bench beside her.

"Of course Dan," she says with a sigh. *A good start.*

They both start to talk at the same time, "Grace, I…", "Dan, I need…", but get interrupted when Jasmine returns, looking aggravated.

Dan looks up at her, clearly irritated. "Yes?" he asks.

"Terribly sorry to interrupt," she says spitefully, "but, we're wanted on Court 5, *now!*"

"But, we just finished a match," Dan says, obviously annoyed.

"Yes, well go complain to the organisers, if you like, but we're on. I'll be waiting on the court," she says, and walks off in a huff.

Dan turns to Grace. "I'm sorry Grace, I have to go. Can we please talk later?"

Grace nods. "Yes, of course.".

Dan gets up to leave, "You won't go until we talk?"

"No, I promise," she replies.

She watches him walk off briskly to where Jasmine and two other people are talking at the net on Court 5. She feels a great deal of relief, but won't allow herself to be completely relaxed. Not yet. She reminds herself that he had said he wanted to talk, and he had made it perfectly clear that he wanted to talk to her as soon as possible. Most people in her positon would find that encouraging, almost proof that it was all going to be alright between them. But, what if he just wanted to clear things up with her? What if sometime over the last seven days he had accepted that it was over between them and just wanted to make sure there were no hard feelings between them? That was the type of thing Dan would do, she reminds herself; always the gentleman.

She sits and watches him on Court 5. He is so handsome, and so very fit. She watches as he plays out a volley with the male opponent. He is so adept at anticipating the next line of play. It's fascinating to watch and almost mesmerising. That reminds her of his eyes; those eyes that she has missed looking into over this last week. Those eyes that always told her how he was feeling. Had he done that a few minutes ago? She thinks back. Perhaps she had been so worried about his actual words that she hadn't paid much attention? Or perhaps he had been guarding his emotions from her. Did that mean he no longer cared? Had he been so hurt by her words that he had put the shield back up, that Darel had told her about on the weekend? She notices

Dan handing the balls to Jasmine to serve. He leans in and says something quietly to her. Grace's shoulders stiffen. Maybe she was right not to celebrate yet. She gets up and goes into the Club House. Where did Johno get to, anyway?

She spots Johno as she enters the Club House. He is leaning back against the wall in the far corner, talking to a girl with long chestnut coloured hair, sitting close by. The girl is laughing and Johno has a big grin on his face. Grace decides not to disturb him.

She notices Sally, one of the tennis organisers, sitting to one side. Sally was always up for a conversation she had learned over the time she had been playing in this comp. She needed a distraction.

It seemed that Grace had chosen the perfect time to offer Sally some company. Sally hadn't had the opportunity to speak to anyone much that night, and she was thrilled when Grace sat down beside her.

She talked about the weather and the effect it had on her home grown garden; she talked about her children and their problems at school; and she talked about her latest find, the recipe for that delicious slice that Valerie Kemp had brought to the last CWA meeting. She said she couldn't wait to make it, it was so delicious. Grace was grateful when several people walked up to ask questions regarding their matches for the night. She swiftly made her exit by going to the ladies room.

She is just about to leave the ladies room a few minutes later when Jasmine walks in. They are alone; behind walls. The first time this has happened.

"Hello Jasmine," she says evenly.

"Hmpf," Jasmine grunts, as she heads into a cubicle.

Grace is about to leave, but just as her hand touches the handle of the exit door, she changes her mind. She notices a chair beside the door and pulls it over and strategically manoeuvers it underneath the door knob, to block anyone trying to enter.

Jasmine flushes the toilet, opens the cubicle door and it about to go over to the wash basins when she notices Grace standing there waiting. She looks at Grace briefly, but ignores her, walks over to the wash basins and begins to wash her hands.

"What do you want Grace," she says curtly.

Grace isn't sure what she wants, why she is doing this. She is slightly perplexed herself. But, why waste an opportunity, she thinks, now it has arrived.

"I just want you to know," she begins, noticing Jasmine has hurriedly washed her hands and is now drying them on a paper towel. "Actually, I recently had a great deal of time to think about things; about you, and about Dan."

"Yes? Jasmine says curtly, heading for the door, but Grace moves in front of her. "What do you want Grace, for God's sake just spit it out," she says, a tinge of worry on her face.

"Ok, I'll spit it out. Jasmine," she begins, but stops. What does she really want to say to her; that she greatly dislikes her, even hates her? For what? Bringing to light the flaws in her way of thinking? For helping her to finally find herself, her whole self and thereafter making her a better person? She looks at Jasmine then, at her pristine attire, despite running around a tennis court for two matches; at her bottle blond hair and perfect make-up, and the mixed expressions on her face. She seems to be annoyed, yet nervous. Well, she had just locked them both in. Was she worried Grace was going to harm her?

"Jasmine, she begins again. "I just want to say - thank you."

Jasmine frowns and glares at her. "What the hell are you on about Grace?" she responds.

Grace feels sudden relief mixed with a sense of power, even though her sincere words were being responded to with contempt. And she suddenly feels sorry for Jasmine. She imagines how difficult it must be to keep up her appearance as a lady, when in reality she was far from being a lady. A lady doesn't have to resort to coercing people to get what she wants. A lady doesn't treat another individual like property, like she does with Dan. And even if she has managed to snare Dan through those unladylike actions, Grace would not descend to those same tactics. She turns and pulls the chair from the door.

Jasmine looks at her questioningly.

"Jasmine, you have helped me realise the truth about myself, and for that I will always be grateful," she says and smiles. Then she reaches across and opens the door. The last thing she sees before walking out is Jasmine standing there with her mouth wide open, in shock.

As she sits watching the grand final of the tennis with Johno and Bernadette, she feels much more relaxed than she expected she would, though still not having talked to Dan. Perhaps Johno and Bernadette's friendly conversation beside her was helping.

Bernadette, or Bernie, as she said she preferred to be called, just happened to be the new administration assistant, at Johno's workplace.

Grace could see they were getting on very well, and she could easily imagine a romance eventually blooming between them. She crosses her fingers for Johno.

From the moment she had left the ladies room, she had felt somehow, free. Like a huge weight had suddenly been lifted from her shoulders. She had thought back on the encounter, and tried to imagine herself ever doing that before. No way, she concludes; she would have been a trembling mess. Hadn't she even hidden in the cubicle in the ladies room at the Club not so long ago? Wow, she thinks, this self-forgiveness thing is so liberating. But, she still needs to talk to Dan. Will she be able to talk to him as confidently?

She looks back at the final match being played; Dan and Jasmine against Darel and Rachel.

"So Grace," Johno interrupts her thoughts, grinning. "Who are you going for?"

"Well Johno. How about you?" She returns quickly.

"We're both in a bit of a predicament here, aren't we?" he says.

"Yep!" Grace leans forward to look around Johno. "What about you Bernie?"

"Well, I get off easy, not being related or friends of either," she says. "I do like the way Johno's brother plays though," she says very diplomatically, and glances at Johno.

Grace nods her head with a big smile and returns her gaze to the match. Yes, she's definitely got her sights on Johno, she decides. Good for her, and good for Johno. She must admit, she's going for Dan too, but having said that, her brother and very good friend, deserved to win just as much.

The match moved very quickly despite the way it remained relatively neck-to-neck the entire way through. And then, as if they had all been in a time warp, it was suddenly match point to Darel and Rachel; with Rachel's serving to Jasmine.

Grace held her breath as Rachel got into position at the back line, paused to look over the net at a position only she could see, bounced the ball, once, twice, three times, and smashed the hardest serve she had ever seen her do. It would have been an ace, had Jasmine not flung herself at it and tipped it. But Jasmine's effort had been in vain.

Darel and Rachel had won! Everyone erupted with delight and Rachel dropped her racquet and ran up to Darel and jumped on him, wrapping her legs around his waist. He laughed at her and kissed her before taking her to the net to shake hands with Dan and Jasmine. The only thing was that Dan and Jasmine hadn't come to the net, because Dan was squatting beside Jasmine who had fallen over attempting to return Rachel's serve. Jasmine was yelling at him, although he was trying his best to help her stand up.

"Ohhh, just look at my leg and my elbow," she was saying. "I can't walk out looking like this," she whined, "with blood everywhere. Ohhh."

By now, Rachel and Darel had walked around to where Jasmine was on the ground. Rachel held out her hand. "Here Jasmine, let me help you up," she said politely. She felt a little charitable now after their victory, especially when she had gotten the better of Jasmine. *That's what you get for being unkind to my friend*, she had been thinking.

Jasmine looks up at the three faces around her and across at the crowd by the Tennis Club, looking very distressed. She is just about to accept Rachel's hand to get up, when all of a sudden Dan picks her up and begins to carry her off. Rachel and Darel follow.

Grace finds it difficult to watch Dan carrying Jasmine. Perhaps she was right not to assume it was all going to work out between them. But, she was not going to allow her emotions to show, here, in front of everyone. Instead, she gets up and meets Rachel and Darel as they come off the court. She doesn't even look at Dan or Jasmine.

"Congrats you two. Wow, what a way to win Rachel. I could never serve like that," she says jubilantly.

Darel and Rachel both smile at her. "No-one messes with my sister, especially when she has a friend like Rachel," Darel whispers when he gets closer.

The three pair of eyes turn to watch Dan carrying Jasmine into the Club House.

"It's ok Grace," she hears Rachel say, at her side. "She was carrying on about her scrapes. Dan just wanted to help her off the court. You know how he is."

"Yes, always the gentleman," she says. "He said earlier that he wants to talk to me before I go tonight. So, if he still does, that will be why I might not be home straight after."

Rachel nods that she has heard, but then Johno comes over with Bernie. He introduces her to Darel and Rachel and they all start chatting about the match. Grace watches and listens to them, but her mind is still on Dan. She hopes Dan hasn't changed his mind. What if he's too worried about Jasmine, and needs to drive her home? She'll feel a bit embarrassed if he leaves without saying anything. Well, she decides, if he does that, then, so be it. At least she will know where she stands. Anyway, there's still time. They need to present the trophy to Darel and Rachel first. That will cheer her up immensely.

Dan walked over and stood by her once the presentation was underway. She couldn't help but feel drawn to stand as close as possible to him. He must be made of magnets she had thought. She just couldn't help herself.

Rachel and Darel are handed the trophy, and she can't stop grinning. She is so happy for them.

"They're made for each other, in more ways than one, hey?" Dan says close to her ear.

She smiles at him. "Yes, they certainly are."

Everyone claps for the final time and then the crowd starts to disperse.

"Are you ready to talk now?" he asks.

"Um, yes, I'll just say goodbye to the others first, ok?"

"Yes, of course, but would you mind coming to that spot by the river we went to before? I can drive you if you like; bring you back to collect your car afterwards?"

At first, the mention of the place where they first kissed gives her hope, but then, perhaps he just wants to ensure they talk in private, and that was one place she knew.

"Ok, but I'll take my car, follow you," she states. She's not going to put herself in a positon of having to be with him long, if he tells her it's well and truly over between them. Although she's now trying to expect it, so she can keep her emotions in check, she knows she's still likely to shed a few tears. And the last thing she wants is for Dan to see how heart breaking their complete breakup is for her.

He nods, with a little smile. "Ok, I'll just say goodbye too and met you in the car park."

# CHAPTER 18

Grace and Dan sit on the same picnic blanket they had sat on the last time they were at the park by the river. And they lifted their knees and wrapped their arms around themselves the same way they had last time, also. Grace feels like she has just experienced déjà vu.

"Brings back memories, doesn't it," he says, though his eyes remain fixed to the water.

"Yes, it does," she says, also looking directly ahead at the water.

He looks up at the sky. "Not a full moon tonight though," he adds.

Grace can hardly stand it any longer. She turns and looks at Dan. He turns and looks at her. "Dan, I want you to know…I'm so sorry," she says with trembling lips. "I…didn't mean to ever hurt you." She looks for his response, but he seems to be weighing up her words. Perhaps he trying to find a way to tell me he's back with Jasmine, she thinks. "It's ok," she adds. "You don't have to worry about me…"

He interrupts. "Grace, I love you."

She holds her breath. "But…?" She adds.

Dan moves closer to her, takes her hand and holds it in between both of his. "But – nothing. I love you. I know you would never hurt me deliberately. I also know you must have had a pretty good reason to call it off between us."

Grace can't believe her own ears. "But…what about Jasmine," she blurts out.

"Yes, Jasmine. Grace, I told you I wasn't going out with her. Didn't you believe me?" he asks with a strained look on his face.

"I did, yes, until Jasmine hinted that you were in an 'on' again, 'off' again, type relationship with her, and that you had kissed her. And then I overheard some people at the Club saying that you would get back together soon…"

Dan gets up, turns around and sits the opposite way to her. He sidles up close, and wraps his arms around her, pulling her close.

"You were saying…" he says with a soft smile. She is looking into his eyes now, and she is speechless. He takes the opportunity to lean down and kiss her deeply.

When they finally stop kissing, they talk.

Grace tells Dan everything that had happened and why she had broken up with him the previous week. She even told him about what had happened at Jannali, except for the letter. It seemed unimportant in the scheme of things.

Dan listened and nodded, sometimes almost distracting her by kissing her gently on the hand, or arm, or even her neck, while she talked. At one stage she had wondered if he were listening to her properly. But when she had queried him about it, he had repeated the information exactly as she had said. So she allowed him to keep kissing her. Besides, she was enjoying it immensely and when she looked deeply into his eyes she had difficulty talking anyway, because she had felt compelled to kiss *him*.

"So, why didn't you come and see me last night?" she asks, pretending offence.

"Ahhh, well I was a bit busy last night," he said, matter-of-factly, which made her curious.

"Do tell," she says half-seriously.

"Ok," he said, moving his mouth away from her neck and sitting up straight. "I went to see Jasmine."

Grace's flinches, and she wonders if she will even be able to hear Jasmine's name without it affecting her in some way.

"It's ok." He notices her nervousness and attempts to reassure her. "Let me explain," he says, taking her hand. "When we…talked that night after tennis, I knew you had been influenced by Jasmine. I've known her a long time Grace; what she's like. She's still the same way she was in Kindergarten; using her father's bearing in the community to get what she wants. I'm not sticking up for her, but her father spoilt her something rotten back then, and he still does.

"Yes, that makes sense," Grace says. "You know, I actually feel sorry for her now, although I still don't particularly like her," she adds, honestly.

"Well, you're a lady Grace. Jasmine pretends she is, but she's far from it," he adds.

"Anyway, I came to talk to you on Thursday. Where were you by the way?"

"I went to the park in town; the one with the ducks and the pond. I just needed to be alone," she says, looking downcast, thinking about how upset she had been.

He knows instinctively she is remembering. "It's ok honey, we're fine now," he reassures her. She smiles gently at his words.

She leads him back to his story. "So, you went to see Jasmine?"

"Yes. You see I went to see her Friday after work, but she wasn't there. Ben, her father, told me she had gone to Canberra for the weekend. He said she wouldn't be back until Tuesday. So, that's why I went to see her last night."

"Hmm, and…? She encourages him.

"I asked her what she had said to you. You see, Jasmine is a terrible liar, so she fussed around for a while, trying to change the subject. But, I finally got her to confess. She also confessed to organising that story she made up about that fella marrying a part aborigine, and how she coerced a couple of her so-called friends to put on that performance near you."

"Ahhh, I did wonder."

"By the way," he has a sudden thought. "I have never kissed Jasmine. She kissed me when I was helping her up after she tripped on a step, last year sometime." He pauses to watch her response.

"It's ok. I believe you. Besides, that was before I came along." Grace wonders at how things seem so much less worrisome when the truth is spoken.

He continues, "I asked Jasmine if she ever had any intention of growing up. I told her that I had never felt in any way romantically inclined towards her and at the best, I even found it difficult to tolerate her as a friend these days. I told her I was in love with you and if she ever said or did anything to harm you or any of your family or friends, I would promptly tell her father. You see Grace, she has always been what you call a 'daddy's girl'. She would be devastated if her father found out she had been unladylike, although I think he has a pretty good idea about his daughter all the same. So, to give her any credit at all, she finally told me the truth, took my response on the chin, and vowed she would never interfere again, as long as I didn't tell her father. She said it was important to her that she and I remain friends. Well, I said that was up to her, but she had better understand that you, my darling Grace, would always come first."

Grace is dumfounded. "I don't know what to say."

"Well as you are obviously speechless…" he says, bending down to kiss her again.

Grace giggles, but stops him with her hand against his chest. "While confessions seem to be the topic here," she begins, ensuring he is listening. "I temporarily locked myself and Jasmine in the ladies toilets tonight."

"You *what?*" Dan sits up, in apparent shock.

"Yes, well I didn't know then, anything about what you've just told me; about talking to her." Dan nods, interested to hear more. She continues. "I don't know whether I was just going to give her a piece of my mind, or what, but I ended up thanking her." Dan's eyes grow wide with surprise. "Yeah, I know it sounds odd, but I realised at that moment, that if she hadn't done what she had, I wouldn't have found what I needed to know. You know – about myself."

"You are an amazing woman Grace, and I'm so glad you've come through all this so much happier," he says caressing her arm.

"Well, you are the icing on my cake, you know," she says mischievously, and giggles.

"Ahhh, I love icing he says, and pushes her back gently to lie down on the blanket. I think I'll start right here," he says, as he begins to nuzzle her neck.

"Dan?" she says, softly, and waits for him to look into her eyes, "I love you too."

# CHAPTER 19

Grace and Mary find a parking space along the street near the solicitor's office. They had made a slight detour earlier, up another street, due to the directions Mary had given. However, they had recognised their error when they had ended up at a park. Mary had pretended it had been intentional.

"Well, I had to use the ladies. Look Grace," she had said pointing to the building in the middle of the park with the word 'Ladies' clearly written on the side. "I good. I direct you straight here, without even knowin', see?"

Grace had agreed that Mary had amazing navigational skills and decided to use the ladies herself. Then she had sneaked a look at the street map while Mary wasn't looking and worked out where they really needed to go.

The solicitor's office was in an older style 1950's brick house, renovated neatly with all the modern accessories befitting a place of business.

Grace was on edge when they walked into the office. She was naturally curious about what this Will entailed, but it was not knowing, *who* it was about, which was the most disconcerting. She just wanted to get in there, get it over and done with, and be back on the road to

Dubbo as soon as possible. Besides, Dan was picking her up to take her to his place tonight. He said he had been practicing his cooking and needed her opinion. He also said that she could drive herself if she wanted to, but he promised he would take her home anytime she wanted, if she would allow him to pick her up. She had finally relinquished her habitual need for independence, and agreed.

Although she is still not feeling completely relaxed, the brown leather seat she is sitting on is very comfortable and watching the fish swim back and forth in the fish tank in the corner has a soothing effect.

Grace thinks Mary must be experiencing the same thing, noticing that she is also watching the fish tank. That is, until she leans over and whispers, "That fish tank is making me want to go to the ladies again. A bit silly puttin' it in a place that makes you wait a long time."

Grace whispers back to her that if she really needs to go she will ask the receptionist where the nearest toilet is.

Mary replies, quietly, "Thanks daughter, but I alright for now."

Grace, and no doubt Mary, will be greatly relieved when the door with the name, David Simon Esq. painted in gold lettering, opens. The door is in clear view from where they are sitting, so both the women repeatedly look towards it, willing it to open.

There is another door around the corner that Grace noticed when she entered the office, but she isn't able to see it clearly from where she now sits. She assumes it must be the office of the partner; the – Parker, of Simon and Parker Solicitors.

She looks over to where the receptionist sits, behind a large desk.

It is made of what looks like oak, sturdy and highly polished. Her vision rises to the top of the desk and she realises the receptionist is watching her, but she then looks down quickly as the door labelled, David Simon Esq., opens. A man wearing a pinstriped suit walks out and looks directly at Grace.

"Ms Taylor?" he half states, half asks.

Grace stands and accepts his outstretched hand, replying, "Yes - and my mother," she says looking briefly at Mary, now standing beside her. She looks back to Mr Simon, but he looks at her expectantly. She suddenly realises why. "Oh, my mother, *Mary Rutherford.* Sorry," she says, a little embarrassed by her omission.

"Very good. Please, come this way." He turns, expecting them to follow obediently.

"Now, it is a pleasure to meet you Ms. Taylor," Mr Simon says, as he walks behind a huge mahogany desk and indicates the two chairs in front for them to sit in. "And, of course, you also, Mrs Rutherford," he adds.

He slides into his chair and looks at Grace. "So, I am sure you are more than ready to find out what this is all about then?" he says with a broad grin.

Mary just looks at him with a deadpan face, and Grace offers a feeble smile. It is obvious they are almost past their limit of patience.

Mr Simon can see that he is not going to receive an answer to his question, so he decides to get straight to it. "Ms Taylor, you have been bequeathed quite a substantial amount of property, assets and money." He looks at Grace, waiting for a response.

"By - *whom*?" she asks firmly.

"Mrs Harriet Bartlett, your grandmother."

Mary gasps audibly and immediately covers her mouth with her hand.

Grace looks at her mother, immediately confused.

"But…," she begins, struggling to make sense of what Mr Simon has just said. But then the penny drops. "Who is my father?" she demands, looking at Mr Simon.

Mr Simon looks towards Mary, and Grace follows his gaze.

"Mum?" Grace looks at her frowning.

Tears have formed in Mary's eyes, and they start to spill down her cheeks. "I …so sorry…daughter," she begins to sob, looking terribly guilty.

Mr Simon pulls Grace's attention back. "Ms. Taylor, I have a letter for you. I'm sure will make things a great deal clearer." He holds out an envelope for her to take.

*Not another letter*, she thinks, as she takes it, looking back and forth from her mother and Mr Simon. "Will someone please tell me who my father is?"

Mr Simon looks toward Mary, but he can see she is far too emotionally upset to say anything. "Ms Taylor, your father was, John Bartlett Jnr, the only child of Mrs Harriett Bartlett, and Mrs Bartlett was…"

"Yes, I know who Mrs Bartlett is, er was. Well I thought I knew who she was. But, I had no idea she was the mother of my *father*." She looks towards Mary, but Mary is refusing to meet her eyes.

"Perhaps, if I may, briefly summarize what Mrs Bartlett graciously left you, her only surviving relative, in her Will?" he asks, looking a little jaded by Mary's soft weeping.

Grace tries to still her racing brain. "Yes, please do. Then perhaps my mother and I will leave."

"Yes, very good. Well, quite frankly, Mrs Bartlett has left you – *everything*."

"Everything? What do you mean? Please explain it in very plain words," Grace asks, unable to think straight.

"All her property, assets and money, as I previously mentioned, which constitute: a wheat and sheep property of approximately forty five thousand acres; the homestead and all buildings, machinery, and of course all the livestock on the property. And also, a bank account with a balance of approximately five hundred and twenty five thousand dollars. Oh, and the homestead was originally built in the early-1800's and is Heritage Listed." He pauses and witnesses the realisation gradually appearing on Grace's face. "Yes, Ms Taylor, you are a very wealthy woman."

Mary gasps again, shaking her head. Grace is now certain Mary is upset because she knew all along who her father was and didn't tell her, along with being overcome by the news of her daughter's wealth.

"Thank you Mr Simon. I think my mother and I had better go now. We have quite a bit to discuss. And," she indicates the letter in her hand…

"Yes, you will find the answers you seek in there. Mrs Bartlett requested I read it in the event of her demise, to ensure it reached its destination." He points to her hand. "You will understand when you read it. She was an astute lady and knew that once I had read it I would be unable to rest until it was delivered into your hands. That is why I asked you to make an appointment Ms Taylor. I made a promise to deliver her letter to you personally."

Grace rises out of her chair and reaches out to shake his hand.

Mr Simon walks around to the side of the desk where Grace stands, now with Mary by her side. "One last thing, Mr Simon…"

"Yes?"

"How did she know my name – Taylor? I only mentioned it to the maid there who went to tell her I wished to speak to her that day. Did she remember it?"

"Oh yes, Ms Taylor, as I said, she was a very astute lady. Now, we will need to stay in communication. I will need to discuss with you at a later date how you wish to proceed, and implement things for you, that is, if you wish to retain my services?" He reaches behind him to take a business card from its holder, and hands it to her, beaming.

Grace drove back to the park after leaving the solicitors office with Mary sitting in the passenger seat, still weeping. She reached over and patted her on the leg. "Mum, it's ok, don't cry."

"But Grace, I should have told you," she said, and began to sob loudly again.

"We'll talk about it at the park, Ok?"

At the park Mary told Grace about her father. She told her that he had taken advantage of her while she was employed at Barons Reach. She didn't tell her about how badly he had treated her, and that it had been more than once. That wasn't something she needed to know. She had already told Grace how Mrs Bartlett had taken her away as soon as she had been born, so it hadn't ended up being as dreadful to explain as Mary had first thought it would be.

"But, why didn't you tell me he was my father to start with Mum?" she asked, still confused.

"Well daughter, I don't think he would admit you were his daughter. You know what I mean...acc..."

"Acknowledge," Grace intercedes for her.

"Yeah. You see, back in them days they never admitted, that's – white man, never admit a child was theirs from an aborigine woman. I was just tryin' to protect you daughter," she said, and the tears started to flow again.

Grace wrapped her arms around her. "Mum, it's ok. I don't blame you. You can let it go now," she said gently.

Mary pulls away from Grace and looks into her eyes. "Do you forgive me for this too," she says broken heartedly.

"Mum, as I told you before - there is nothing to forgive. You did what you had to and you have shown me nothing but love. Please don't cry."

Mary sighs deeply. "You a real good daughter Grace," she says wiping her eyes, finally getting her emotions under control.

"Now, I need to read this letter," Grace says, reaching into her shoulder bag. She pulls the letter out and looks at her mother. "Would you like me to read it aloud?"

"If you wants to daughter. Up to you, but – yeah, I would like to know what the old dragon had to say."

Despite all the upset of the day, Grace smiles. "Mum, she was my grandmother you know, and she's made me a wealthy woman."

"Yeah, I know. Hmpf. See what that woman got to say for herself then," Mary says, indicating the letter in Grace's hand.

*\*\**

*Mrs Harriett Bartlett*
*Barons Reach*
*Bathurst NSW 2795*

*3 January 1979*

*Dear Grace,*

*When you receive this letter I will no longer be alive. I have requested this letter to be passed on to you by my solicitor, David Simon, of Simon & Parker Solicitors, Bathurst. He will be of enormous assistance to you if you decide to retain his services. He has been my solicitor for many, many, years and he is loyal and trustworthy.*

*By now you will know that I am your grandmother. You will also be surprised to know that I knew who you were the moment I met you on that day you came looking for your mother. I hope you found her. She was a good employee, and I had not wanted to end her employment with us, but I had no other option at that time.*

*Your father, my only son, was unfortunately quite disappointing. He was often lazy and regularly imprudent and never really in my affections. When he died at the result of a car accident in the month of July, last year, I felt little sorrow. You may find that to be rather sad, but I only speak the truth. If I am to say anything in his favour, it would be that he possessed a stubborn streak which could have proved to be an asset. It was such a shame that he couldn't understand that.*

*It is, however, that same stubborn streak which I saw in you, when you visited that day. You walked into my sitting room, and although I instantly saw your mother, I very quickly became aware of your father's boldness. You have your mother's beauty, that is without doubt, and her resilience. You would not have come into my sitting room if you had not had those qualities you inherited from your parents.*

*You reminded me so much of both of them at the one time; that flawless face of your mother's, and the stubborn chin of your father's. You refused to leave until you were satisfied. I could see it in your eye, just like I often saw it in my son when he wanted something badly. But when you coerced me to tell you, by that wonderful attempt at blackmail, I nearly cried for joy. My granddaughter was a fighter. At that moment I knew I would leave Barons Reach to you.*

*I am glad I had the opportunity to meet you, if only for a short while. I know you will be good for Barons Reach. Honour her and care for her as if she were your daughter.*

*Your grandmother,*
*Harriett Bartlett.*

***

On the way back to Dubbo, Mary spoke little, and Grace almost felt like she was in a trance as she navigated the road ahead automatically. By the time they arrived at the flat at Dubbo, they both looked exhausted. It had been an emotional afternoon.

"Would you like a cuppa Mum, before you head out to Jannali?"

Grace asks as they get out of the car.

"No thank you daughter. I just want to get home to Don."

Grace walks around the car to her and embraces her. "Mum, are you ok?" she asks with a worried look on her face. "I'm sorry this was such a big shock to you."

"Daughter, I ok, don't worry. I happy you find out these things. I can put them to rest now too. And you gunna be ok, with ownin' that property an all. Just wait till I tell Don," she then adds, brightly.

Grace feels better now, knowing her mother is showing a bit of her usual spirit. She helps her into her car and waves her off. She then goes into the flat to find Rachel preparing tea and tells her the news.

By the time Dan arrives to pick her up, she is feeling a great deal better. It seemed the initial shock of it all had finally started to wane.

She told Dan about the Will as soon as they arrived at his home. He was amazed by the story, and happy for her that she now had more answers about her family. He then announced that he was a very clever man for falling in love with a very wealthy woman.

Grace then reminded him that he had fallen in love with her *before* she found out she was wealthy.

He replied that she had made a good point, and could she please remember that always, because he didn't want her to ever forget that he fell in love with the girl who was lost, but found more than she could ever have imagined.

# EPILOGUE

Grace looks around at each member of her family as they stand by the burial site at Barons Reach.

There had been an enormous number of documents and paperwork she had had to steadily work her way through in her grandmother's office. It had taken her several trips from Dubbo to Barons Reach, and many long nights at the homestead before she had finally managed to get through it all.

When she had come across the document she now holds in her hands, she had instantly called Mary and told her about it. It was one of those moments she would never forget, because Mary had actually been speechless.

She had not had any difficulty in finding the burial site, although there had been nothing in the paperwork to indicate where it was located on the huge property. She had known she had been guided to it. And she had felt an incredible uplifting of her spirit; a powerful energy that surrounded her as she stood in reverence before it. She had known she had not been alone at that time.

From the moment she had found the document, she knew she held a story she had to share, not only with the Wiradjuri people, but with all Australians. She promised herself she would do everything she could to ensure the story would be remembered by as many people as possible.

She knew the story would affect people in many different ways. To some, it would be nothing more than a transcription about a part of Australian history. To others, it would be the catalyst for healing on many levels. But, everyone needed to know about it all the same.

Grace imagined its effect on each member of her family:

For Mary, it would strengthen her quest to continue to educate those in her family about the Wiradjuri ways, so that those who fought for the Wiradjuri nation would never be forgotten. In her own quiet fashion, Mary had already been fighting alongside her ancestors. However, the document would reinforce the truth she had successfully passed on to Grace; that there was no shame in being an aborigine, instead, there should be nothing but – pride.

Then there was Don. She remembers the diaries he had shown her of his grandfather soon after she had arrived at Jannali. He had told her that his grandfather's diaries were accounts of his great-grandfather's life as the first white settler in the Dubbo area. He had proudly told Grace how his great grandfather had befriended the aborigines in the area. He would be saddened by the story because his ancestors had lived in peace with the aborigines, and he had married a Wiradjuri woman too.

Of all her family, it was Darel who shared the closest resemblance to her own situation. Their white ancestors had both held prominent positions within Australia, at Dubbo and Bathurst. But, they were also just as strongly connected, through their Wiradjuri mother, to the

Wiradjuri people who preceded settlement. Darel and Grace knew how to live in peace with both races, and they had proved this by their relationships with Rachel and Dan.

Then there was Rachel. From a very early age, she had embraced the Wiradjuri culture, seeking to learn all she could from Mary and Darel; a white girl, respectful of the Wiradjuri ways, with a bonded love for the land. Her marriage to Darel was again, proof, of the ability of both races to come together in love.

Dan, the love of her life: A man who held no claim to aboriginal heritage or as a descendant of any prominent white settler in the area. Yet, he was now an integral part of Grace's dual world and its rich history, through the simple act of having fallen in love with her.

It would also be with Dan's support and his connections in the modern world that Grace's ideas of providing a way for 'lost' Indigenous children to reconnect with their heritage and their families would come to fruition. And, through Grace and Dan's efforts, along with Mary's assistance, Baron's Reach would become in many ways, a haven for healing.

*\*\**

On 1st January 1980, Grace, Dan, Mary, Don, Darel, and Rachel, all made their way to Barons Reach for an important occasion: The first reading of the document at the burial site.

The Wiradjuri burial site at Barons Reach, marked by the Bathurst District Historical Society in 1954, with a monument plaque, and a stone axe-head, recorded as the 'resting place of Windradene'.

Grace looks at the document in her hand and begins to read:

*Windradyne, also known as Saturday, Windrodine and Windradene, was born in 1800 and died in 1829. He was a warrior and resistance leader of the Wiradjuri nation, in what is now central-western New South Wales, Australia.*

*Windradyne led his people in the Bathurst Wars, a resistance movement by the Indigenous Australians against the invasion of their lands by the British settlers.*

*Hostilities between the Indigenous Australians and the British settlers began just a few months after the First Fleet arrived in January 1788, with casualties on both sides occurring as early as May 1788.*

*While the early confrontations generally involved few combatants and were relatively rare, as the British population increased and spread further out from Sydney, they came into contact with increasingly large numbers of Aborigines of different tribes and nations, and the frequency and intensity of the conflicts increased. These conflicts would come to be known as the Australian frontier wars.*

*For the first twenty-five years of British settlement, the Wiradjuri's land in the central part of New South Wales remained isolated from the settlers, due to the intervening barrier of the Blue Mountains.*

*In May 1814, the exploration party of Blaxland, Lawson and Wentworth found a route across the mountains, essentially by following existing Aboriginal trails. From a peak later named Mount Blaxland, the explorers claimed to have seen 'enough grass to support the stock of the colony for thirty years' on the other side of the mountains – the Wiradjuri country…*

\*\*\*

Grace looks up after reading the last page of the document. All members of her family are still looking at the burial site.

Don has his arm around Mary, and she is brushing tears from her eyes. Darel and Rachel are holding hands, in deep thought. Dan, standing beside her, now reaches for her free hand. He squeezes it gently.

Mary is the first to break away from looking at the burial site. She walks up to Grace.

"You did real good daughter. The ancestors and me be right proud of you. I might not like that old grandmother of yours, but it good she leave Barons Reach to you. She probably even be turnin' in her grave, knowin' now how she help the Wiradjuri people." A smile tickles her lips at the thought, and Grace can't help but smile also.

Dan whispers in her ear. "My little lost girl, just look at her now?'

*Coming Soon...*

**Barons Reach**
Book 3
The Dreaming Series

www.ingramcontent.com/pod-product-compliance
Lightning Source LLC
Chambersburg PA
CBHW020614180626
46810CB00007B/2766